INHIBITIONS
AN ANTHOLOGY

I0616815

Featuring:

Keisha Ervin

with Rose Jackson-Beavers

Cecila Edwards

Kareem Tomblin

P. O. Box 2535

Florissant, Mo 63033

Copyright ©2013 by Prioritybooks Publications

Edited by:DOCUVERSION LLC

Cover Designed by Brittani Williams and Majaluk

ISBN 9780989650236

Library of Congress Control Number: 2013921300

Manufactured in the United States of America

For information regarding discounts for bulk purchases, please contact Prioritybooks Publications at 1-314-306-2972 or rosbeav03@yahoo.com. You can contact the author at: www.prioritybooks.com

INHIBITIONS

Published by Prioritybooks Publications

Missouri

Table of Contents

From all the authors:

We give thanks to all our friends, readers and family members for all your support. We love you all!

"Mommy, I'm doin' hard time,

And I'm not stress free.

That's why I'm in your presence;

I need for you to counsel me. "

K. Tomblin

INHIBITIONS

by Kareem Tomblin

ONE

"I wonder can you keep a secret?"Dr. Goodson said to me, soft and sexy like, as she poured herself a hot cup of vanilla banana cappuccino.

"Whatchu mean, you wonder?Of course I can keep a secret," I shot back.

Her back was facing me, giving me perfect view of her permed out hair, which hung down to her mid back and laid over her milky-white, satin button-down blouse. Her knee-high skirt was charcoal gray, fitting ever so sexy and tight. So tight, I could clearly see her panty line as it hugged her luscious and juicy booty. A sight that reminded me in no uncertain terms of what I had been missing. Some coochie!Her three-inch heels highlighted her sexiness all the more, exposing her muscular calves and making her booty look more plumped.

"You can keep a secret, huh?"

I figured she wanted to hear me affirm as she turned and faced me, standing a little distance away.

"Doctor Goodson, I'mma gangsta. A true one at that. We don't tell secrets. So, like I said, yes I can. "

"You're a gangster, huh?"

"Not gangster, Doctor Goodson. Gangsta. See, you take the 'er' off of it and put the 'sta' on it. Gangsta. You feel me?"I schooled.

"Bobby Lamont Jackson, pullease. "She rolled her eyes and poked her juicy lips out, which were painted with ruby red lipstick. She then licked cappuccino from around the mouth of the cup in her hand, looked at me with her almond eyes through the thin framed glasses that sat perfectly on the bridge of her semi broad nose, and said, "You've been locked up for how long, Bobby?"

"Almost six years. You got my file over there. You know how long I've been away from society. "

"Almost six years and you still talking about you're a gangsta, as you put it. Boy, you ought to stop it. "

I lifted my hands slightly and shrugged my shoulders. "It is what it is, I guess, Dr. Goodson. "

"No. It's what you make it," she corrected.

"Hey, it was you who told me that change don't come easy, right?"

"Right. But don't try using that as an excuse to justify igno-rance, Bobby. You've had plenty of time to get that street mental-ity out of your system. How many times have I also shared with you in our sessions that ignorance is a cure for nothing?And how many times have I shared with you that just because you were a street person yesterday, don't mean you have to continue that curse and be one today or tomorrow?"She shot back, trying to make me think. She then rested that fat, juicy booty of hers on the edge of her desk and sipped her cappuccino, waiting on a response from me. "Oh, don't get quiet now, Mr. Gaaangsta. "She stretched the word, smiling.

"Naw, I'm just thinking about what you just said, and you know what?You're absolutely right. Eventually I'll get to the point where all of that street stuff is out of me. I'm just not there yet," I assured, taking a seat on the dark blue cushioned sofa a few feet from her desk.

Dr. Goodson sucked her teeth like she was a ghetto girl from the hood.

"Mmmm, hmmm," she muttered. "If being in prison and attending these private sessions hasn't helped to at least somewhat change your mind, then I don't know what will. Anyway back to my question. Let's get back to it, because I really need to know the absolute truth. "

"Cool, let's get back to it, because I want to know what's on your mind. "

She sipped her cappuccino again and licked around the top of the cup. "Puedes mautener un secreto?"

She asked if I could keep a secret in Spanish. She loved speaking a little Spanish on my ass.

"America is turning bilingual. You need to learn Espanol," she had once said to me in a prior session.

"Naw, what I need to do, Dr. Goodson, is to learn to keep my hands off of cocaine. How's that for my Spanish?"I had replied laughing.

"Definitely keep your hands off of that," she shot back, waving me off.

Now here it was she was speaking Spanish again on me, wanting to know if a brotha can keep his mouth shut. I didn't know what she was up to, but I knew it was something. Why?Because that was Dr. Goodson. She was sweet and down to earth like grass, but she was always up to something.

She and I had become pretty cool and straightforward with each other over the twelve months I had been in her one-on-one private counseling sessions here at FCI Bennettsville, A Federal Correctional Institution located in Bennettsville, South Carolina.

FCI Bennettsville wasn't my first prison. Prior to coming here, I was doing time at a penitentiary. Unlike the penitentiary, though, where the hardest of the hardest criminals are held —murderers, big mob bosses, crooked CIA officials, gang chiefs, and the like. FCI Bennettsville was a laid-back less hostile environment.

I don't even know why the government sent me to a high security prison like the penitentiary. I was only twenty years old at the time, and my only charge was possession of crack cocaine. I had gotten busted with a quarter kilo of coke. Nine stankin' ass ounces of crack.

"One hundred and twenty months," the old cracker judge had said when he sentenced me, looking down on me from his chamber.

"A hundred and twenty months?"I shouted. "Damn, Your Honor, you act like I shot and killed some fuckin' body!"

I could count well, so I knew that one hundred and twenty months equaled me being locked away from society for ten years. My mother literally fainted when she heard the judge hand down that sentence on me. She had to be carried outside for fresh air.

I flipped the judge a bird. "Fuck you, Your Honor! And fuck the government!" I started to turn around and moon the judge, but I remember hearing that he was a Catholic. Bending over and showing my red ass might excite that cracker to the point of him getting a hard-on underneath his black robe. The marshals had my hands cuffed in the front anyway. One of them even aggressively grabbed me by the arm to escort me out of the courtroom.

"Getcho cracka-ass hands off of me, muthafucka!" I vehemently spat while twisting and turning. That's when two others came to assist the one I twisted my arm away from. They all escorted me out the courtroom while I was kicking and screaming.

"Fuck all y'all muthafuckas! Y'all always hang a nigga for nothing!"

I felt I had been judicially lynched! And I was extremely angry. That anger followed me straight to prison. I hadn't been behind steel doors and concrete walls for two weeks before I had to check a Ru'Paul homo-ass nigga's temperature.

"What the fuck you keep looking at me for, bitch? Huh?" I had snapped while sweeping the cell floor.

The sissy disfigured his face, snaked his neck, and sucked his teeth. "Since when was it a crime to look at someone? Whatchu got a complex?" The sissy bitch shot back, standing in front of me with his hands on his hips.

"I ain't got shit but a dislike for a nigga perpetrating like he a sista. So put your eyes on a nigga who go that route before I bust your punk ass!"

His eyes got big and his mouth opened wide. He then turned around, bent over, slapped his own ass cheek, and said, "Dammit, bust it then. "

That's when I put my prison-issued, leather steel-toed boot up his ass as hard as I could. I then broke the broomstick in two and started swinging.

"Muthfucka...don't...you...ever...ever...play...me...like. . . I'mma punk lover!I...will...goddammit...kill...kill...you!"I viciously beat him until I saw blood everywhere!I thought I had killed the sissy because he was out cold. It took four officers to get me off his ass. And six months of solitary confinement were my reward, and a one-year loss of my telephone and visitation privileges. When I got out, nobody fucked with me. They thought I was crazy. I wasn't, though, I just wasn't the one for the bullshit.

I managed to keep somewhat of a level head for the next three and a half years I was in the penitentiary. I then got shipped here to FCI Bennettsville on good behavior. Still unable to shake being judicially lynched, I elected to sign up for psychotherapy. That's how Dr. Goodson and I met. I knew I liked this chocolate sweetheart when the first thing she said to me as I was signing up for her one-on-one private session class was "You've got the prettiest eyes I have ever seen. What are they, blue?"

"They change colors. One day they're blue, the next they're green. Don't ask me what makes them change colors, though, because I have no idea. "

"Well, they are really beautiful. "

"Thanks. I appreciate the compliment," I said, cheesing from ear to damn ear. After I signed up for her class, I walked away, out of her presence. But when I looked back, I noticed she was watching me.

I began attending private sessions with Dr. Goodson. We had sessions three times a week. She and I discussed feelings and thoughts about everything. Particularly, situations that if not handled in a positive manner could lead to stress, worry, depression, and even suicidal thoughts and actions.

"The more you get off of your chest about what you are going through, Bobby, the better you will feel afterward," she always expressed in past sessions.

Our sessions were held in the mornings. That was the only thing I hated. I hated that because mornings in prison were the worse for me. This was because I would awake every morning with a hard dick!Doing so without being able to roll over and put it up in a wet, warm vagina where it belonged had me mad at the world!My only hope of my morning hard-ons subsiding was masturbation. Sometimes I would have to masturbate two and three times. But when I did, I felt so much better. Absent masturbating in the mornings, I would have to walk around with an inflated snake in my pants, which was very uncomfortable. Trust me.

Dr. Goodson's method of counseling was cool, though. So I continued coming back. The thing I loved most about her method was that she never allowed me to share my heart and mind with her without her sharing hers with me.

"Bobby, I used to not be able to stand guys," she had shared with me in a prior session. "They made me feel like I was the most unattractive girl on the planet!They were always calling me derogatory names like Miss Fatty, Blacky, Ugly, Sister Four Eyes. In college the names continued. Donkey Butt, Miss Lil Melons, and so on. "

"And how did that make you feel, Dr. Goodson?"I would say after listening. I would ask her that because that's what she would usually ask me after I shared something with her that I disliked.

"It made me feel ugly and not wanted...like God had made a mistake in creating me. "

"So what changed that perception, Dr. Goodson?"I further questioned out of curiosity, seeing that she was a very beautiful black sista. A little heavy, but beautiful in my eyes nonetheless.

"Not what changed my perception, Bobby. More like who?My father. He assured me that guys are a trip, especially when they are young. He taught me, among other things, that guys are stimulated by what they see. If a girl is not a light skinned Halle Berry or a Tyra Banks supermodel type with a slim waist, and you know, nice firm hips and a fat booty, then most guys will not want to pay much attention to them. You know how y'all guys are, Bobby. Y'all will call a good intelligent girl ugly. But as my father assured me, beauty is in the eyes of the beholder. He said that it is also skin deep. So, I just learned to love myself and see myself as a beautiful woman. After I learned to do that, I paid little attention to immature comments coming from immature guys who simply just needed to grow up!"

"Oh, you definitely right. I can't even dispute you. Your dad dropped some real jewels on you. In the hood, we like to say: never let a dime get in the way of a dollar. You are a dollar. Other people's opinions——especially the negative ones—are just dimes. Small change in other words. "

She smiled. "Bobby Lamont Jackson, you something to deal with, boy. I don't know whatchu doing in prison. You shoulda went off to college somewhere. "

"Everything isn't for everybody. I'mma leave it at that. "

I had met no one in the Federal Bureau of Prisons more straightforward and real than Dr. Goodson. Sista kept it 100 with a brotha every session. According to the rules of the Federal Bureau of Prisons, though, staff and inmates were not allowed to share personal information with one another. It compromised institution security. I sensed Dr. Goodson didn't give a crap about the rules. She wasn't a loose cannon in total disregard of the rules either. She just knew that inmates were human beings just like she was. The only difference was inmates got caught doing their wrongs.

Dr. Goodson wasn't a correctional officer either. She was a psychotherapist who worked for an agency that was contracted by the Feds. So in truth, she didn't have to answer to no one but the head of her agency. The private session that she had set up was just that. Private!She didn't let the warden or no one else from the prison's staff know of her method of counseling. Neither would she allow me or anyone else to talk about what went on in our sessions.

"What goes on in here, Bobby Lamont Jackson, stays in here, no exceptions," she had told me from the start.

Later, after getting to know Dr. Goodson better, I broke down in all honesty and told her the reason I disliked that our session had

19

to be conducted in the mornings. Eight o'clock in the mornings to be exact.

"Dr. Goodson," I said, "I wake up every single morning in this place with a bonafide hard-on and wanting to have sex. "

"And how does that make you feel, Bobby?"

"Like a damn pervert!"

"Why?"She stretched the word, smiling.

"Because…because my hard-ons leads to me pouring myself over pornographic books, which leads to me masturbating. I be wanting the real thing, though. "

"Were you having a lot of sex when you were out, Bobby?"

"Every day, Doctor Goodson. Every single day. In the mornings especially. That's what I miss the most. Why you think I some-times come to our sessions with that mad look on my face that you be telling me to wipe off? I be wanting me some. "

When I shared that in a prior session with Dr. Goodson, she removed the arm of her eyeglasses from her mouth, got up from sitting behind her desk, and said, "Get up. "

I got up as she requested, unsure why she asked.

She reached for my hand, which I yield to her without consent. She placed it on her booty and said, "Squeeze. "

"Squeeze?"I said with a raised brow. "Are you sure, Doc?"I got instantly nervous.

"Boy, Bobby, squeeze my damn booty before I change my mind. Now go ahead. "

Without further delay, I grabbed a handful of her juicy booty and squeezed as much of it as I could grip in my hand. Lord have mercy that thang was soft as cotton! My dick was immediately awoken from its slumber.

I released her booty. I didn't want to be greedy. I prepared to sit back down, but she reached for my hand.

She said, "I didn't tell you to remove your hand from my booty. Now put it back. Matter of fact, Bobby, grip both of my buns with your hands. "

Again, I complied. She could feel my nervousness through my touch.

"Just relax, Bobby. Close your eyes and relax with your handsome, red, curly hair, tall self. "

Dr. Goodson was a short sister. Five-five to be precise. I was 6'1. She looked up at me while placing her hands on my chest and said, "Now take your time and close your eyes like I said and squeeze what you been missing. "

I closed my eyes and pressed my fingers into her softness. I rubbed and squeezed her goods until I damn near lifted her skirt.

"That's it, baby boy. Do you. You have my per…permission," she said so sexy like and in a low voice tone.

As she permitted, I took my time and enjoyed caressing her goods. I could feel her breathing hard on my neck.

She whispered, "God made woman for man, Bobby. Absent a man experiencing what a woman has to offer, he is most miserable. "

"Yes…yes…he…is," I said softly, in between squeezing her ever-so-soft buns. But when the cobra in my pants began poking out and touching her midsection looking for a wet, warm target to strike, I reluctantly removed my hands from her booty. I saw her smile and removed her hands from my chest.

"Now, Bobby, how did doing that make you feel?"

I wanted to say "It made me feel like easing you up out of your panties and putting your legs over my shoulders and fuckin' you until you tell me to quit!"Instead, I said, "Doing that, Dr. Goodson, made me feel human. "

Dr. Goodson's eyes took a trip down south to my hard-on. I was so aroused and couldn't hide it.

"I'm glad doing that made you feel human, Bobby," she said. She then cracked a smile and walked back to her desk. "That's the power of touch, Bobby. " She took her seat. "Touching is very therapeutic. "

When that particular session was over, I went straight back to my cell and released myself, thinking the whole time that, this couldn't be true.

Well, that was two days ago. Now here I am up in Dr. Goodson's office and she's asking me can I keep a secret?Fuck yeah, I can keep a secret. I didn't run back to the cats here in prison and tell them about her juicy booty she let me rub and squeeze on. It wasn't any of their goddamn business anyway.

I watched Dr. Goodson as she placed her hot cup of cappuccino on her desk. It was a polished ebony desk with a wooden nameplate that read Dr. J. Goodson written in italic letters next to the title Psychotherapist. A light blue folder containing my file, a writing pad that she take notes on, and a black and gold ink pen that was given to her as a gift from the warden sat on the desk as well.

She removed her eyeglasses and walked over to me. I was leaning back on the comfortable sofa with my legs parted, the thug way!

She leaned over and planted her hands on each of my legs, just above my knees. She tongued her lips, I assumed to ensure they weren't chapped, while inhaling and exhaling hard through her nostrils. Something was up. I saw it in her eyes as they squinted and pierced into mine.

"So can you, Bobby?Can you keep a secret?"

"If it's dealing with anything involving class, Dr. Goodson, of course I can. Told you I was a gangsta, and that true gangstas don't tell. "

"It has everything to do with this private session of ours. "She licked her lips.

"Then spit it out. Talk to me. What is it, Doc?"I shot back, looking her in her eyes to let her know that I could be trusted.

"I want you to fuck me with that big dick I saw bulging through your pants the other day when I let you squeeze my booty. Don't ask me am I serious either, because I am. Now get ready," she said, letting up off my legs.

I started unbuckling my belt and unzipping my fly. I dropped my pants and underwear in one single motion. I was about to get me some pussy, and as far as I was concern, there was nothing else needing to be said.

TWO

"Before you fuck me, Bobby, I want you to lick my pussy,"
Dr. Goodson said, lifting her skirt and easing her panties down.
She turned around directly in front of me, sitting on the sofa, and
bent over like she was a stripper getting paid big bucks to do so.
Nothing but ass and a fat hairy pussy invaded my face. She was at
least 200 pounds of black sexiness. Thing is, I had never in my life
licked a fat girl's pussy before. When I was out in free society and
getting that drug money, all that came at a nigga were chicks that
looked like they belonged in beauty pageants. They were the only
type of chicks I put my tongue on and my dick up in. So I hesitat-
ed when Dr. Goodson asked me to do that.

"Go ahead, Bobby Lamont Jackson. Lick it," she said, looking
back at me.

"Why you want me to do that, Doc?I mean, why can't I just
fuck you real good?"

"Because," she stretched the word. "Because I don't just like
big dicks. I like getting my pussy licked. Now come on before the
time for our session run its course. "

Dr. Goodson's ass was burning up for some loving. I didn't
know who wanted it more, me or her?Not wanting to blow a gold-
en-ass opportunity, I parted the hairy lips of her goods and tongue
danced up, down, and around her clit.

"Oh God yes, Bobby, that feels good," she moaned.

I tasted her sweetness until she was soaking wet between her legs. I then placed my middle finger inside her wet and warm love tunnel. I did so only to lubricate my finger so that it could slide into her anal cavity with ease.

"Unh. "She tensed up and moaned as I eased my finger in and out of her tight asshole slow and gently while simultaneously circling my tongue over her swollen clit. I heard her take air between her teeth in pleasure and saying, "Gosh, Bobby, your…fin-ger… feels wonderful in my ass. Don't take it out, please. "

I continued fingering her asshole, slowly until I had a better idea. I closed my lips down on her clit and started humming.

"Ah!" she screamed.

The deep vibrations coming through my lips pleased her clit. I fingered her in the ass faster as I hummed. She had pretty muscular legs, but they weren't strong enough to support her under the feeling she was now receiving. They began quivering profusely.

"Uh…uh…uh…uh…Bobby…I'm cumming!And…it…won't… stop," she screamed with her mouth open wide looking down at the floor. She said, "I have never been fingered in the ass like this while getting my clit hummed on. "

I could tell it was the truth by the way her whole body was shaking.

My face was glazed from her sexual eruption. I wiped my face and finger with her panties then bent her over the sofa with her ass tooted high in the air, and beat her pussy up like I was mad at her for not giving it to me sooner!She reached her hand back and placed it at my midsection to prevent me from penetrating too deep and hitting it too hard.

I grabbed her hand and put all of my manhood as deep as I could get it inside her. "Bobby, you...gon'...gon' get...me...preg...pregnant," she said as I hit it fast and hard. She continued moaning and groaning while I spanked that pussy. I watched her big black booty slap against my midsection.

"Damn, this pussy good," I said with my eyes shut. She was good, wet, and warm. I found it difficult to come out of her!Neither did she want me to. My dick agreed, because it would not soften. So I positioned her on the floor and placed both her legs over my shoulders and proceeded to lay pipe to her that way. A surprise prevented me from putting in serious work, though.

"Oh shit!"She said, looking past me. "How long have you been standing there, Dr. Beasley?"

Dr. Beasley was a short Caucasian blonde, the same age as Dr. Goodson, thirty-five. She looked just like Pamela Anderson Lee. She even had the nice, big titties and a fat little ass. She was a psychologist working next door.

"Long enough to know that you are about to get escorted off of this prison compound," she shot back.

Dr. Goodson was now trying to put her panties back on. I was so in shock that my pants and underwear were still down, and my dick was still hard and pointing forward as ifit were giving directions!

Dr. Beasley put her walkie-talkie to her mouth, an indication that she was about to notify prison staff members of what she had just discovered.

"Please don't radio me in, Dr. Beasley. I can explain," Dr. Goodson said.

"What is there to explain, Dr. Goodson?You're up in here with an inmate's cock buried in you, like you're in the Bahamas or somewhere on vacation!"

"I know, but—"

"But what?I'm supposed to turn a blind eye to your behavior?You're supposed to be counseling, not fucking!"

"I know, Dr. Beasley, and I'm busted, but please don't radio me in. I'll do anything for you. Anything. "

I just looked on—still in shock—with my dick out and hard. I was about to pull my pants and underwear up, but Dr. Beasley looked over at me and said, "You better not move a muscle!"She then focused her attention back on Dr. Goodson.

"So you'll do anything, will you?"

"I'll do anything. I swear… You name it," Dr. Goodson said, trembling harder than she was when my dick was in her.

"Since you said that, then here's what I want you to do—"

"Whatever it is I'll do it," Dr. Goodson interrupted.

"Well, I want you to suck my pussy. "

"Suck your pussy?"Dr. Goodson was not expecting that request.

Dr. Beasley looked over at me. "Young man, did you just hear what I requested of Dr. Goodson?"

"Yes, ma'am. I heard you," I humbly said.

"Then if you heard me loud and clear, I know she did. Now, for the second and last time, I want you to suck my pussy or else you're leaving up out of here in cuffs. "

"Okay, okay, okay...I'll do it. "

"I thought so. " Dr. Beasley lifted her skirt.

THREE

Dr. Beasley lifted her skirt and removed her panties. Well, not panties, more like leopard thongs!

"Suck my pussy just like I saw that inmate sucking yours from the back," commanded Dr. Beasley.

Dr. Goodson did as told.

"And you, inmate, come over here and sit in front of me on the floor. "

I too followed her command. When I did so, she gripped my dick, which was still hard, and placed her whole mouth over it. "Damn," I said.

Dr. Goodson was sucking Dr. Beasley's pussy and looking at her as she graced my hard-on. The look in Dr. Goodson's eyes— seeing how much I was enjoying this white girl giving me head— suggested that if she had a gun she would have shot the fuck out of us both!I closed my eyes and inhaled air through my teeth as Dr. Beasley deep throated my dick.

"You like that, Mr. Inmate?"

"I, I, I love it. No one has ever blessed my dick as you are doing. Thank you so much. " I moaned as she tightened her jaws and circled her tongue around and around the head of it like she had a PHD in blow jobs.

Dr. Goodson again looked up at me as if to say, Negro, what

the fuck you mean, nobody has ever blessed your dick as she is doing? Did you forget that you just slid that dick of yours out of this good pussy?"

Dr. Beasley then said something that blew my mind. She released her mouth from my pipe, looked back at Dr. Goodson, whose face was wet from her vaginal juice. "That's enough of you back there. I want him to fuck me now. "

Dr. Goodson looked at her as if to say, White bitch, Bobby wouldn't dare put his dick up in you!

Dr. Goodson must've forgotten that I was in prison and horny, because if I was reading her right, her thinking was so wrong. My dick was now harder than ever and fucking this chick until being ordered to stop was now my assignment, per her request.

"Lay flat down on your back, Mr. Long, juicy cock," Dr. Beasley said.

I lay back with my hard dick pointing northward.

"Oh, and by the way, Dr. Goodson, you can stand over there in the corner and watch," Dr. Beasley said.

Dr. Goodson walked over to a corner, leaned herself against the wall, and crossed her arms. I saw her roll her eyes behind Dr. Beasley's back. Dr. Goodson definitely didn't like this white woman telling her what to do, or stealing her dick. But she didn't want to get ratted on, so she reluctantly complied with all of Dr. Beasley's orders and so did I.

"Have you ever had a white woman ride your cock?" Dr. Beasley locked eyes with me.

"Never," I replied as she eased her way on top of me.

With her hand gripping my hardness, she placed it between her pussy lips. "Neither have I ever ridden a black man's cock. Always wanted to, though. You've got a big one. "

"Is that right?"I said as she eased herself down on it gently.

"Uh-huh," she whispered with her eyes shut tight. "Lord, you've got a nice one. "She started traveling up and down it like she was on a seesaw.

I looked over at Dr. Goodson as this white freak was motioning herself up and down my pipe. The look on Dr. Goodson's face said, Bobby, you better not be enjoying that white bitch!I didn't want to disappoint Dr. Goodson, but this white chick's pussy was like Dr. Goodson's. It was wet, warm, and hugged my dick perfectly.

"Grip my ass cheeks," Dr. Beasley said while simultaneously slinging her long blonde hair to the side of her shoulder.

My fingers sank into the flesh of Dr. Beasley's ass cheeks. She was as soft as a pillow filled with feathers.

"Yes, now fuck this pussy!"She said with her arms stretched and hands buried on my chest.

I lifted her by her ass cheeks and glided her up and down on my hard dick. When I would bring her body down, I would lift my hips and pound myself into her.

"Yes," she screamed. "I love it when you do that. Please keep it up. "

Dr. Goodson was watching every bit of my dick penetrate in

and out of this white chick's hot pink hole. Dr. Goodson was my friend. I hated for her to see me working my jimmy up in this white chick. What was I to do, though?Not fuck the bitch?I had to in order to save Dr. Goodson's ass and my own, as well as for the pleasure.

"Yes, fuck this hot pussy. "

"You love this eight-inch-sugar dick up in ya, Doc?"I penetrated her pussy deeply.

"O' God yes, wish I could take it home and sleep with it in me!Lord knows I...I...haven't stopped...stop cumming since... since I sat...sat on it. "

I saw Dr. Goodson shake her head. She was unappreciative of Dr. Beasley taking over our private session. Tears started flowing from Dr. Goodson's eyes. I sensed it was literally killing her to see my dick planted up in this white chick and making her feel good. I saw her clamp her teeth together and make a mad face. A face that said, you better hurry it up and remove your dick from this bitch,' cause you been up in her long enough, Bobby Lamont Jackson!

Before I could even consider doing what I sensed Dr. Goodson was thinking, Dr. Beasley eased up off of my dick and said, "Bend me over Dr. Goodson's desk and fuck me from the back. "

I checked the expression on Dr. Goodson's face after Dr. Beasley made that statement. Her look said, No the fuck this cracka-ass bitch didn't ask Bobby to bend her over my desk?Shit, it's enough the bitch getting some dick on my office floor!Bobby, your ass better refuse!

"Why don't I just fuck you real good right here on the floor, doggy style?"I didn't want to offend Dr. Goodson any further.

"That's not what I want," she shot back, letting me know who was running the show. "I want you to fuck me bending over Dr. Goodson's desk. Now if you don't want to do it, I'll radio in and have you locked in solitary confinement for breaking the prison policy code, fucking Dr. Goodson. "

"Bitch please!"I said under my breath, before aggressively bending her over. I lifted her skirt, smacking her hard on her ass cheek and thrust my dick hard up in her.

"Ooh!"She screamed and tried to run.

I gripped each side of her waist to prevent her from doing so and started pounding that pussy in and out. "You-gon-take-all-this-dick," I spat. "It-is-what-you-want, isn't it?"I grinded deeper and harder.

"Lord yes. Hurt the muthafucka!"She cried out. "Hurt it!"

"Why?" I shot back, humping.

"'Cause, 'cause I've been a bad girl and need to be taught a lesson. Punish me!Punish this hot pink cunt. "

"I placed myself all the way up inside her as deep as I could go. I held my dick in her just like that. I wanted her to feel it throbbing deep within her. I then started hitting it fast.

"That's it, Daddy. Oh yes!"She screamed. She started throwing her pussy back and shaking. "Please don't take it out," she said.

I was about to cum hard until I was aggressively pulled by the back of my collar and snatched out of the pussy.

"Ah, why you stop and take it out?"Dr. Beasley said. She then turned around when she heard me stumble to the floor.

"He took it out, bitch, because he didn't have a choice!"Dr. Goodson snapped, gripping a thirty-inch black steel flashlight.

"No fuckin' body, dammit, disrespects my desk!And, dammit, nobody sucks and fucks a dick that belongs strictly to me. Nobody, bitch, absent my permission!"Dr. Goodson blanked out and attacked her.

Dr. Beasley was hollering, scratching, and kicking, but she was much too small to render a prevailing counterattack. It only took seconds before the little defense she offered came to holt.

"Now look at you, bitch, fucked yourself to death!"Dr. Goodson spat. Her once milky white blouse was now heavily stained with undisputed evidence of foul play. So was the flashlight that dripped the DNA of Dr. Beasley onto the shiny marble white office floor.

Dr. Beasley's lifeless body lay slumped over with her skirt up, pantiless. As Dr. Goodson stepped over her, she looked over at me with an inflated nose and biting down hard on her bottom lip. She tightened her grip on the bloody flashlight and headed toward me. I was in the process of pulling up my pants and underwear, but was cut short the moment I saw Dr. Goodson's arm and hand cocked back to render me a death blow with the flashlight.

"No!No, Dr. Goodson," I shouted, shielding my head and face from the brutal assault I saw coming.

BEEP!BEEP!BEEP!BEEP!

That's when I awoke breathing hard and in a cold sweat. I had never been so glad to hear my alarm clock. The midsection of my boxer briefs was wet. I had had a wet dream. It was one of the many I had while serving my time here in prison. But never had I had one that turned nightmarish. And thing about this dream was every damn thing in it was exactly how it's been for me. I was in for possession of drugs. I had ten years, which was running me loco. I was in a federal correctional institution located in Bennetts-ville, South Carolina, and I attended private psychotherapy sessions with a very beautiful, chocolate, sexy lady name Dr. Goodson. She and I were cool as ice, but never had we been sexually involved as we were in my dream. I couldn't understand it. Why was I having some of the best sex in my life with her and with the white chick who busted our ass fucking like rabbits?I didn't know. Neither could I lay in bed thinking about it any longer. I had to get up, wash my ass, get dressed, eat me some breakfast, and prepare for my real session with Dr. Goodson.

* * *

I entered her office at eight o'clock on the dot.

"Oh, good morning. How are you, Bobby?"She greeted me in a cheerful-like manner, while pouring herself a cup of cappuccino. The banana-flavored aroma arrested my nostrils, instantly putting me in remembrance of my dream.

"I…I don't know how I feel this morning. "I took my seat.

Her back was facing me. Just like my dream, she had on a white button-down casual blouse and a charcoal gray, tight, knee-high skirt. A skirt that her juicy booty looked so good in.

"Whatchu mean by 'you don't know how you feel this morning,' Bobby?You ought to be glad to be attending this session of ours this morning. "She sashayed over to her desk, rested her juicy booty on it, took a sip of her cappuccino, and waited for me to respond.

I rubbed my hand over my short curly hair, while at the same time inhaling and exhaling hard, causing my jaws to inflate. "I just don't know how I feel. That's all. A male thing, I guess. "I shot back unable to make eye contact with her. I couldn't do it, because I was too busy eyeing the way her booty graced the edge of her desk. I wanted so badly for her to lift her skirt, ease her panties down, and sit on my dick from the back as she was doing to that desk of hers.

She placed her cappuccino on her desk and walked over to me. She locked her sexy almond eyes with mine. Her brows were arched and so ladylike. She reminded me of a dark skinned Monique, who played a key role in the movie Precious.

My heart started beating fast when she looked into my eyes. She bent her face down closer to mine. So close that if I had moved forward an inch my lips would have been touching hers.

"You should be glad to be attending this session, Bobby Lamont Jackson. You know why?"She said soft and sexy.

"No, I don't," I replied, unlocking eyes with her only to view her cleavage that I could see perfectly, as she was bending down. She had some nice lil' melons. They were not too big. Just a handful for a brother to suck on and enjoy.

"You should be glad to attend this session because I have something for you, Bobby. "

"You do, huh?"

"Mmm hmm. "She licked her lips. "I sure do. "

"And what would that be?"I said, feeling my nature raising.

"Just what you like. "

"Just what I like?"

"Mmm hmm. "

"Dr. Goodson, you know how I am. I keep it real, and I know you do too. I haven't had what I like in years. I like getting my dick sucked and fuckin' my lady until she tells me to stop. That's what I like, Doc. No bullshit. "

"And, I like getting my pussy licked and letting my man have it his way inside me rough and raw. "

"Really?"I shot back nonchalantly.

"Yes, really. Thing is, I don't have a man. "

"How long have you had that problem, Dr. Goodson?"

"Long enough. Now… all I want to know this morning, Bobby, is can you keep a secret?"

My mind immediately flashed back to my dream, and what the outcome of it was. "I don't know, Doc. It depends on what it is," I replied after thinking about it.

Dr. Goodson took her hand and did something she had never done before. She caressed my jimmy until it was throbbing hard. She took in air through her teeth with her eyes slightly shut, and said, "I want this log of yours to keep my fire burning. Can you give me some without running your mouth about it?"

* * *

Jelisa hit her thirteen-year-old brother upside his head and snatched her book from his

hand, killing his chances of finding out what would happen with Bobby and Dr. Goodson.

"What I tell you about sneaking in my room and reading what belongs to me without my permission?Huh?Now this is grown-folk type of reading material. Don't let me catch you with it in your hands again!"She shouted in her brother's ear. His name was Abdul Ra'heem, straight A student in school, but one who had already once got caught reading Hot Chocolate in Full Figured 5. He was sent to the principal's office for having a book with dirty, sexual content in it while attending his eight-grade class.

His principal wanted to suspend him for three days, and would have had not his big sister, Jelisa, taken the blame for leaving her book in his book bag one night while she was in need of using it for something, like to store that book, her calculator, and some other book on accounting at the spur of a rushing moment. Thing was, out of curiosity, Abdul Ra'heem began reading the book and couldn't put it down. He'd been sneaking in his sister's room reading her books ever since.

Now, in the middle of a good story, his sister busted his ass with her book titled Inhibitions. Engrossed in the story too deep and wanting to know what would transpire next between Bobby and

Dr. Goodson, Abdul Ra'heem snapped on his sister for abruptly interrupting his read.

"Damn, I don't see what's the big deal, Jelisa!It's just a book!Won't you let me finish it?"He reached for the book so that he could pick up where he left off, but it was to no avail.

Jelisa placed the book behind her back with speed, gripping it tight in the process. "I swear, Ra'heem, if I ever catch you going into my room, messing with my belongings, I'mma beat the stank off your lil' ass!You hear me?"She warned with her finger pointed at his forehead and with her teeth clamped together tight in anger.

Ra'heem sucked his teeth and waved her off. "Just like a bitch to trip over small shit!"Under his breath, he shot back with an attitude.

"Whatchu call me?"She followed behind him and hit him upside the back of his head. "I don't care anything about you catching a little attitude. When you get grown enough to read these types of novels, then you come holla at big sis. Maybe then I will let you read a lil' sumthin' sumthin'. Might even turn you on to one of my fine friends. Until then, focus on school and stay in ya place! And stop trying to be grown before your time. "

"Man, whatever!"Ra'heem shot back, going into his bedroom, slamming the door behind him, and locking it. "Wanna preach, get a church!"

"I got your man… You lil' punk!"She shouted, hitting his door with her open palm before stepping off.

Ra'heem slumped down on his bed with only one thought

echoing loudly in his head:Get that book back, and do so as expeditiously as possible!It would be a mission that he would definitely seek to follow-up on. The only obstacle in his way was his big sister Jelisa. If she had anything to do with it, her book, Inhibitions, would not be in his hands anytime soon.

CAN'T GET
ENOUGH OF YOUR LOVE

By Rose Jackson-Beavers

ONE

She moaned, "Yes, right there. Oh yes, that feels really good. Harder, harder, yes, right there, baby. Damn, yes. Fuck me, baby. Ah, shit, yes. "

The king-size bed was so soft that every time Jared pumped into his new conquest, her supple body bounced back into him.

Princess felt every inch of Jared's penis. Normally, she would never be able to take a dick so big, but the brother knew how to use his thang. It had to be at least ten inches because she could feel it thrusting deep inside her stomach. But damn, she might never be able to fuck again after this time, because he was digging and thrusting up in her like she was the best lay he'd ever had.

She withstood the pain because the pleasure was delightful, but for right now, he was twisting her back out. She kept trying to use her Kegel exercises to tighten her vagina muscle to keep him nestled inside of her. Every time he pumped out it felt like he pulled her intestines down with him. She held on as best as she could, even though she was having a hard time trying to concentrate with the thrusting he was putting on her.

"Come on, baby, roll them hips," Jared demanded. He grabbed her by the heel of her right foot and boosted her leg up over his shoulder. "You like this dick, baby? You know you do. Show me how bad you wanted it. " He drove down hard into her then gently pulled his penis halfway out so he could view her pretty face and see her reaction. Just like he thought, she was going crazy with passionate screams.

"I want it bad, baby. Give it all to me. Please baby, go deeper. "Rolling her hips as if she was in a hula hoop contest, she squeezed her vaginal muscles again to hold him in and to tighten her grip, for she would be devastated should he slip out of her wetness.

"Oh yeah, yeah, damn, you got some good pussy. "

She felt him stiffen inside of her as his member swelled and filled every inch of space inside of her lubricated walls.

"Ah," they both screamed as orgasms rippled through their bodies.

Kissing him passionately, she did not want it to end so she started kissing him and rubbing his body. She lightly rotated her hips on his flaccid penis as she lay beneath him throbbing. She flicked her tongue in his ear while she whispered; her breathing heavy from being worked over. Yet, her words were flooded with sexiness and nasty talk. "I need you to fuck me again. I have put your dick on notice and I want it to move. "

They kissed and she sucked his tongue. They twisted and rotated in the sheets as they swapped the sweetness of their lips. As they tongue danced, she thought about why and how they met. She had long wanted to meet him after hearing about him. He was 6'3", rich, and—based on rumors—had a good sex game. He was a handsome African American. She heard in the past that the many women he dated had a difficult time letting him go when it was over. They followed the breakups with stalking, crying, and vandalism. They would fight, scream, cry, and harass whomever he was with at the time. In the end, Jared ignored them until they simply faded by the wayside.

In addition, he was oversexed. He could not seem to be faithful to anyone because he needed sex to function. Sex guided him and he had the money to get it anywhere. He found that women were drawn to him because of his money. Yet, he didn't mind because each of them wanted something from the other. The women wanted his money and he wanted some pussy.

Jared made his money in software development. He also developed video games; he created one called Build A Car; it was flying off the shelves across the country, as young teens tried to learn the inner workings of designing a car with reasonably priced gadgets. Jared lived in a mansion in Ladue, but he also had homes in Atlanta and a summer home in Hawaii. He traveled often and he lavished his conquests with expensive jewelry. For those he had more than sexual feelings for, he would gift them with beautiful clothing and jewelry, but if he had an emotional attachment he would do more. One young lady he helped her start her own business. Today, Jennifer was a successful media and marketing mogul. Often he would slip back to visit Jennifer. He would probably never get Jennifer out of his system, unless someone took her place, like the one laying underneath him. Long story short, the lady lying underneath him—with the juiciest pussy he had felt in a long time, was one he wanted to see again and again.

Princess Gina Mays was a news reporter for a local news station that was very popular. In the evening she served as a reporter, but her main function was anchoring the midmorning news. Her audience was huge, over two million, so many people had an opportunity to see her. She was recognized everywhere she went. She was a good person but had one downfall: she loved good sex but didn't want a commitment. Actually, she was considered a nymphomaniac. She craved sex to calm her constant need for orgasms. In addition, she wanted to feel different men with each sexual episode.

She was also spoiled, and usually got whatever she wanted. This was why she set her sights on Jared. Princess heard about him all over town. After all, St. Louis was large enough to get lost, but small enough that everyone knew you. Especially if you were popular, on television, successful, and had money like her. She had a decent salary so she wasn't into men with money. Hard dicks, though, that was a different story. Jared was successful and had plenty of money. She wanted to feel his dick all up in her to determine if the rumors about his dick and the smooth way he used it were true.

Princess heard about Jared while hanging out in St. Louis. She heard he was packing in the sex department, and he could twist a cherry stem into a knot with his tongue. Damn, when she saw him that was all she could think about—his tongue slowly manipulating the stem of a cherry and wondering if his tongue could do those same kinds of tricks on her vagina. Now that he was feasting on her body, she was satisfied, at least for the moment. She knew that, soon, her vagina would start to twitch for attention.

As she lay in his arms, he gently pushed a strand of her hair behind her ear. "I definitely want to see you again. "He bent down and kissed her.

Their tongues danced and she felt herself becoming wet again. She thought about how he wanted more time with her, but all she wanted was the sex and then she would send him back to his woman. Jared's reputation preceded him. Everybody knew that no matter what he would return back to his real lady, the one sporting a huge yellow diamond around town. She decided to enjoy her moments with him and send him back home. Why should he care?He did the exact thing to other women he was bedding. So deep in thought, she almost missed what he was saying.

"Damn, girl, I love your pussy. I ain't going anywhere. Shit I'mma make you mine. "

Jared slowly started to roll his hips again until she felt his penis rise against her throbbing vagina. As she lay underneath his warm and supple body, she thought about how she had finally conquered him. It actually didn't take long. She sucked on his earlobe and whispered to him how good he made her feel. As they rocked their hips in sync with each other to prepare for round two, she thought about the day she met this muscular, walnut-colored, dark-eyed hunk.

"Jared!"She had paused as she considered calling out his name again. "Damn," she said as she looped her lips and called his name. "Hey, Jared!" From the moment she saw those eyes, she knew it was him. He had the longest eyelashes she'd ever seen on a man. Also his eyes were dark but had a twinkle, which sparkled in his eyes and made you feel as if you were seeing exploding stars. She had seen him before but it wasn't the opportune time to say anything to him. This time, baby boy was by himself. She had been watching him for a while. Well, truthfully she had been stalking him. Princess had to have that brother. She knew he had a steady woman and was in love based on the rumors. Her name was Tameka. She heard his lady was real pretty, but guess what? So was she.

Princess had never been afraid of any bitches. No matter how bad and no matter how pretty they were because she had it like that. She could have any man she wanted. "It's how you play the game and not how the game played you," Princess always said. So being 5'5", 120 pounds with a small waist and definitely cute in the face, she decided to take what wasn't hers. This was going to be easy for her because Jared Jamison Johnson had a bad habit. Dude was a habitual lover and she knew that for a fact. She knew he was twisting out this girl Terri's back any time he wanted too. Jared and Terri had an on –and-off again relationship. They dated early on before he met Tameka. Terri's ass was trifling because if he really wanted her, he would have never left her for Tameka.

Princess did really respect Tameka because she was his woman, but not enough to stop wanting to sample her man. In a way, the chick was smart as hell because she was wearing his ring and was engaged. Tameka reminded Princess of what her dad used to tell her when he would say, "Why should the man buy the cow when he can get the milk for free?"She totally understood her dad, but dig this. She wasn't trying to buy the cow, she just wanted to sample a little bit of the steak. Yeah, sister girl wanted to feel the dick. Plus, she thought the damn milk comes free with all that dick anyway.

Anyone listening would want to know how she knew about

Jared's dick. She heard all about it sitting under a hair dryer at Elegance Beauty Salon that Terri owed. You know what happens at beauty shops, right?Nothing but gossip and great hairstyles!While you waited to get your hair primped, crimped, and styled, it was easy to find out who was fucking who and anything else you wanted to know. Terri was really stupid. One thing Princess learned was never ever talk about your man's dick because if you are bragging about how good it is, someone like her would just want to find out all about it. You know if it was that good, then she wanted to see herself. At least that was what Princess planned to do.

Another thing was this:Men like Jared liked to hit and run. It took some special shit to keep him coming back. So apparently Terri could make him forget about his fiancée for a minute, but she couldn't make him leave her. Fucking Princess, though, might change that because she was not a simple bitch. She was intelligent, wise beyond her years, and would hurt someone for playing with her heart. Princess believed that once Jared sampled her goods, he would want to come back too. Truthfully, though, she was just like him. She wasn't interested in being anybody's woman. The last man she was in love with couldn't handle her sexual appetite. As a matter of fact, John Mason was the man who made her look for sex on the outside of their relationship. She thought about the first time she sought sex outside of their relationship. She had always heard a bad man could make a good girl go bad. Now she was bad!But the funny thing about that was how she loved being the one who was bad and making all the moves. Still, every now and then, she was reminded of the first night she started craving for more dick. The video clip of how it all started played on the screen of her mind like it was yesterday.

TWO

John was hitting her from the back. "Yeah, baby, this shit is so good. "He was hitting her hard just like she liked it. "Princess, damn, girl, what are you doing to my mind and my body, baby?"

Princess was on the verge of the biggest orgasm. She could feel it build-up from her thighs to her stomach. It was like a storm that stirred before it boomed out of control into a full-blown tornado.

"Oh, damn, girl it's so good, yes," he shouted and it was over. "I'm so sorry, baby. Your sex is so good I couldn't hold back. "

Next thing she knew he was snoozing. That pissed her off so she shook him awake and did everything to arouse him.

Pushing her away, he said, "Settle your ass down. I'll hit you off with this dick tomorrow. You's a greedy-ass bitch. "

As she showered to leave the house in search of some good, hard dick, she cried. First, he called her a bitch, and next he didn't feel she was worthy enough for him to wake up to hit her off again. He left her totally unsatisfied. So she did what she had to do. She went to a bar and met a man, talked to him awhile, went to the bathroom and Googled his name in her cell phone. When she saw that he was a legitimate businessman, she felt safe enough to invite him to a hotel room. That man whipped her into a frenzy.

She called him often too.

* * *

Snapping out of her almost trancelike state, she waved her hand and called him again. "Hey, Jared. " When he looked around, she smiled and said, "Yeah, you, baby!" The street was busy with downtown traffic. People ambled by in their business clothes: men in their fancy shoes and suits; women in new suits with miniskirts accessorized with their running shoes, socks, and designers purses and briefcases. Princess had to wait until a cluster of folks walked past and cleared a line of vision to the man she wanted to feel inside her.

"Do I know you?"Jared gave her the once-over.

"No, but I hope you want to. "She gazed at him. It appeared dude was about to get smart with her so she said something to make him smile. "My name is Princess, and I want to wave a wand and sling some of my magic stuff on you. "

"You do?"He tilted his head to the side and rubbed his chin like he was considering it and was impressed to be selected. He eyed her up and down from head to toe, landing his eyes on her plump breasts.

She watched him watching her. He was licking his lips, sort of like LL Cool J, the rapper, does. His eyes fixed on her breasts like he was putting his imprint on them. He smiled and licked his lips like he wanted to taste them. See, a man like him couldn't resist her goodness. Truth be told, she really felt she was better looking and finer than both Tameka and Terri. Even though they were both some bad-ass chicks. But if you put both of them together, they didn't have shit on her.

"Yeah, baby, Princess needs her magic wand today and you

must give it to me. "

"Damn, girl. " He took a step back and placed his hands on his legs while leaning slightly to the side. "I like a woman who goes after what she wants. You pretty as hell, not as pretty as me, but I can work with you. "

He relaxed his leg back and she saw he was bow-legged. Next he pasted the prettiest smile on his face. This man was cocky as he could be. But Terri said that when she was bragging about his big dick.

"Girl," she had told everybody in earshot, "that dick is like an Anaconda snake. " She stretched her hand out to indicate how long it was.

Again, what a fool!So Princess looked at those pretty-ass teeth and said, "Straight up, I want to fuck you, and after this one time, that's it. No matter how good my stuff is to you, I'm not looking for a relationship. I just want to hit and run. " Like him, she was stuck on herself.

She gave him a taste of his own medicine. Word was that he was not only cocky but also arrogant; however, the brother told you straight up that it was nothing but sex so if you got your feelings involved, that was on you. Now that was a confident brother to be telling a lonely woman something like that before even having a chance to twist her back out.

He laughed at her. Dude was cheesing hard. "Oh, it's like that?"Rolling his hand across his pant leg, smoothing out a little wrinkle that was barely there, he wanted her to see all of his goodness. Though there was no lint, no wrinkles, or dirt, but there was one thing there, Mr. Snake. That boy was coiling. Terri never lied. Dude was packing. He had to be about nine-and-half to ten-inches long. Thing was, she wanted desperately to feel how thick it was. So she whispered, "Follow me, bad boy. " She grasped his tie and used it to pull him behind her. He followed without hesitation.

Walking to her Lexus 450, she swung her hips from side to side as sexy as she could. He jumped into his BMW convertible and followed her. She took him straight to the Four Seasons Hotel, which was only about ten minutes from the Scottrade Center. As she drove, she occasionally glanced up at her rearview mirror checking to ensure he was still tailing her. She licked her lips as she felt her vagina throbbed.

Princess chose the Four Season hotel for two reasons: she wanted to be comfortable when she was wrapped in this brother's arms, and because she knew that men like Jared loved expensive things. After all, he was extremely wealthy, owning several companies. The hotel, as usual, was busy since it was only three blocks from the Mississippi River. It was also less than one mile from the new gaming center, Lumière Place. She already had a room booked there because she had a guest coming in from out of town later that night. By then, she would be through turning brother man out.

They reached the hotel and parked. She waited on him to catch up to her. As they walked, he wanted to chat. "What do you do, Princess?"

"I work in the media arena. "

"I thought that was you. Wanted to see if you were on the up and up! I'd never forget a pretty face like yours. Plus, I don't have time for games either. "

"Is that why you are with me right now going into a hotel? You know I'm a stranger to you. "

"But, baby, you turn me on. Plus, I feel like I know you. "

"Really?"

"Yeah, seriously, it's not always that I do something like this. "He couldn't even hide from telling that lie. His eyes bounced around when he made that statement. Hell, this man followed her, a stranger, to a hotel. So what that told Princess was that his dick led him, not his heart. Now Tameka may have his heart but Princess was about to have his dick.

They rode the elevator to the third floor, and he followed her to Room 3004. She keyed the door with her card and they walked in. He was following her when she quickly turned around and kissed his soft, sexy lips. Damn, Jared could really kiss. Not too sloppy and not too dry. Just right! That was her first turn-on. They kissed and he started taking her clothes off. He was eager and was kissing her on the lips, neck, and in the chest area. She was wearing a black miniskirt that buttoned down the front. He expertly removed it. Every time he unbuttoned one button, he would take a second or two away from kissing her. As her dress dropped to the floor, he whispered, "You got a pretty-ass body. " He admired her by smiling, and he even kissed her on the shoulders.

She stood in all her nakedness with only designer pumps on. She grabbed him by the collar and kissed him again and again. Then she started stripping ole boy down. First, she removed his shirt, and then she kissed and sucked one of his breast buds. Jared smelled so good with his woodsy and musk scent. The cologne was her favorite. On a man it gave him that rugged and unkempt scent that turned her on more. She took off his belt and felt inside his boxers. "Umm," she moaned as she smacked her lips together. "Damn, boy, you are packing. " She massaged his member up and down. She wanted to see how thick and long his penis was. She gripped it and squeezed gently.

He sighed as he reared back on his sexy bow legs. Pulling her close to him, he kissed and sucked her neck and pecked a trail of kisses along her face and chest area. She briefly broke free to check him out. She observed the ripples in his stomach. His six-pack appeared to be rippling back and forth as his breathing became more labored.

Princess wanted his dick. She wanted it fast too. She took control and pushed him onto the bed and pulled his pants down. Soon, she had him naked and was admiring his body. She could eat his ass, which was exactly what she was going to do. She bent down and sucked and licked stiff boy until Jared was gently trying to release her mouth from his piece. He was hard as a board of wood and ready to enter her, but she wanted to keep the control. This was different for him; he was used to being the aggressor and the one in the driver's seat.

He stood at the end of the bed shaking as she licked and sucked him. He gently pumped into her wet and warm mouth. As he thrust deeper and harder, she moaned. Jared's penis felt good in her mouth, and she couldn't grip it tight enough. She was holding on to it because he was too excited, pounding his dick toward the back of her throat. She was trying not to gag. Suddenly he pulled away.

"Damn, girl, who taught you how to give head like this?" He let out a breath, trying to stabilize his breathing. He took another step back to regain his composure because his legs were shaking so hard and he didn't want her to feel like he was losing control.

She pushed him back on the bed onto the down-filled pillows and was about to climb on him for the ride of her life when he turned her over.

Grabbing her face and holding it steady as he looked into her eyes, he said, "I would know your pretty ass from anywhere. I watch you every night on the news. Don't think I didn't see your pretty ass in Terri's shop. I see you there every time I fly in. Not only that, I peeped your ass following me too. "

"So what!" she said. "When we finish fucking, forget you ever met me. "

Before she could say anything else, he was kissing and slurping on her neck, leaving little red marks on her easy-to-bruise skin. Then he kissed her all the way down to her most prized possession. He licked her pussy so good that she could feel the orgasm building down in the bottom of her feet and as it began to move toward her center. He stiffened his tongue in pushed it in and out of her like a Jack in the Box toy, jumping out of the closed part of the box. Jared turned her over and licked her vagina from the back.

Moaning loudly, "I'm coming," she screamed. She felt her liquid explode out of her like a volcano eruption releasing lava. She had never felt anything like she was feeling. His tongue was like magic. He caressed and vibrated on her clitoris until she lost control. She could feel the sticky flow easing down the inside of her thighs. After he lapped up her juices, he twirled her back over, entered, and stroked her so slow and deep; she was whimpering and groaning like she had lost her strength.

"Damn, girl, your shit tight. I'm gonna fuck you real good. Believe that!"

All she could say as she tried to collect her breath was "I don't do this with just anybody. But I want you to fuck me hard. "

Knowing this Jared pushed deep into her. He thrust in and out of her while she shifted her body to match his pace. Then he turned over again and pulled her on top, which helped him to enter her again. They fucked hard and long. He squeezed her butt tight to prevent himself from slipping out. She fucked him good because she wanted him to remember how good her pussy was. Jared gently lifted her up and out of the bed with his dick still inside her and grabbed her ass to secure his hold on her. He held her tightly as he pumped hard up into her.

"Damn, boy, you feel good as hell inside me. "

Then he gently pushed her back onto the bed and pulled her to the edge. This fine motherfucker fucked her so long doggy style that she had two more orgasms, and then his body tensed. He whispered, "Oh, baby. " And it was over.

When he released her, she dropped gently onto the bed, pulling him into her arms. She glanced over at the clock and saw that they had been fucking almost an hour.

Jared got up and removed the condom, the second one of the

day, and pulled her up into his arms. He picked her up. Princess wrapped her legs around his waist as he carried her into the marble bathroom. Releasing her and allowing her to stand on her own, Jared twisted the shower faucet to turn the water on. Then he tested the water to ensure it was at the right temperature. He picked her back up and carried her into the marble glass-walled shower to finish what they started. His stamina was amazing.

The bathroom was gorgeous with a mirrored-embedded TV. He put Princess down once they were in the shower, kissing her as he backed her into the black-and-white marble wall. Placing her arms above her head while he sucked her nipple, he tore the wrapping from a fresh condom. She helped him roll it on. Once done, he rammed her, digging his dick into her with force. Princess took a deep breath as his huge penis throbbed and thrust deep up into her. The warm water hit their bodies, spraying them everywhere, they both exploded. Weakened, they kissed as he held her up to prevent her from sliding down the wall—due to her legs giving out from such a powerful release that siphoned her strength.

After they finished their time together, he had nerve to say he wanted to see her again.

But she whispered, "I'm not interested in a relationship. "

"Guess what, pretty Princess, I'm not either. I got a woman and I'm deeply invested in her. Call me, baby girl, when you want to fuck again. You see, baby girl, I am not married yet. "Fortunately for her, she rarely called him. He was the one doing all the calling and begging to see her. Not wanting a relationship but loving his sex, she accepted his offer to have sex several more times. Then she decided his skills were so good, she couldn't see him again. There was no way she would allow herself to fall for him.

* * *

Weeks later as she sat in her office her phone rang. She picked it up and hoisted it to her ear so she wouldn't have to use her hand. "This is Princess. "

"What's up, baby girl?"

She immediately recognized his voice. "Jared, why are you calling me?"

"You know exactly why I am calling!"

She tapped the keys on the keyboard. When she looked at the story she was writing, she had unconsciously written Jared has good dick. She laughed.

"What's so funny?"

"You don't want to know. "She deleted the words out of her story and saved her document and turned away from the computer screen. "Let me get something straight. You were simply a fuck. So why are you calling me?"

"You know I want to see you again. You don't put that thing on a man and think he won't call again. " He breathed hard. "I can't get you out of my mind. I'm thinking about your pussy all the time. "

She heard breathing and changed the phone from one ear to the next. "Jared, you were just a three-night stand. I had my fun, got my fuck on, and guess what, sexy, it's over. I have a man. "She never heard his comment because she laid the phone back into its cradle. She smiled and said out loud, "Damn, these men want to hit women with their sex and run, but they can't handle getting hit back with the same thing. But, Jared, go fuck your fiancée. You are great, but I don't hang around to get my feelings all hurt. "She turned to face the computer and typed The End. Yeah, Jared, the end, brother, she thought.

THREE

Jared couldn't shake Princess out of his mind. She captivated him like only one woman ever had. He leaned back onto his big, burgundy leather chair, grabbed his humidor chest, opened it, and clutched a Stradivarius. He lit the cigar and took a gentle pull. He inhaled the aroma of the Havana seeds. Relaxing, he closed his eyes and leaned onto the soft leather headrest. His mind wondered to Princess, a lady he couldn't seem to get out of his head.

When she walked, her phat ass jiggled and bounced up and down with a special jerky movement. While her butt swayed from side to side, he felt as if it was speaking to him. Her long black hair bobbed to the front and blew gently in the wind like she had her own personal hair fan. He was caught off guard with her beauty. What she didn't know was he had been checking her out before she ever laid eyes on him. For the past year he had been watching her anchor the nightly news. She was so gorgeous with her small prissy nose and bright doelike slanted eyes. He had spotted her while flipping the channel on his television more than a year ago. But he was the man!He would never let a soul know he was that smitten by sight only. Shit, he was a player. Plus, he had asked Tameka to marry him. He had being dating her for more than two years. She was a teacher. A conservative, quiet, easy-going woman and she was beautiful and secure. No trouble to him, so he decided she was the one woman who could give him babies without a bunch of problems.

But Princess was fucking all that up. After the day she spotted him and they fucked like there was no tomorrow, he knew she was still imagining him planted deeply inside of her; likewise, he had been thinking constantly about her. Hell, did she know he used her face to fuck random girls? Is it possible to fall in love with a face on a TV screen? He also wondered would he even want to be with a woman who so boldly asked him to fuck her.

Damn, thinking about a woman like this was so unlike him. He could have any girl he wanted. On the side, he had four women he laid with frequently. He never wanted for sex. Whenever he needed sex, all he had to do was summoned whichever one he had a taste for; and, yes, they came running. All he had to do was pick up the phone and dial their number, and as if they were sitting there waiting fully dressed they would be there. There was no excitement in available booty. If women only knew it was the chase that got the man. Hadn't they heard that song Atomic Dog? I'm a man and we like chasing cat, simply put!

Jared's father, Cecil, had died five months before his fifteenth birthday in a car accident. For a long time his mother, Gwen, suffered and went into depression. She had bouts of crying fits. Some mornings she couldn't get up. So her best friend came to help her. Jared had great memories of his dad; Jared spent a lot of time with him when he was working. Cecil told his son that having money brought access. He taught Jared how to save and invest money. They would spend days flipping through the Wall Street Journal looking for stocks to purchase. His dad was an engineer with an airplane company. When Cecil died he left them well off, which was where Jared got the money to continue making invests.

With money came access, and he was able to bed as many women as he wanted to. But Princess's pussy hit the spot! It felt good and familiar, like warm and toasty. He draped his leg over the arm of his leather chair and laid his head back onto the headrest and reminisced as the white cigar smoke floated into the air.

He was fifteen and horny! His mother's best friend had come to visit from out of town. She had to be about thirty-four. She was cute with a short haircut that framed her face like a pretty picture. She was about 5'5," a little shorter than he was, and she had a petite frame but a thick booty that set high up like she could carry a glass of water on it without spilling one drop. She had chocolate satiny skin with a face so youthful she could pass for a teen. But she was all woman. He knew that by the way his dick responded whenever she entered the room; he wanted her in the worst way. Although he had been jacking off regularly, since she came to their home he found himself doing it twice a day. He also regularly tipped to her doorway, which was at the opposite end of the hallway where his mom slept. He would peeked through the keyhole and watch her oil her body after she showered and he would grip his big dick and masturbate. One night while he was peeking through the keyhole on the old door, she spread her thick thighs apart, lay down on the bed facing the door and massage her pussy in plain sight. She was fingering herself as he watched. He grabbed his dick and imagined himself inside of her. As he visualized that, he got hard and he found he needed to release himself, so he began to groove with her. As he masturbated he lost himself and twisted the door knob, falling into her room. She looked over his shoulder to see if anyone had seen what happened but all was clear.

"Come in and shut and lock the door. "

He did as she said and made sure he locked it too. He strolled over to her and she grabbed him and kissed him using her tongue. "Damn, boy, you can't kiss worth a fuck. "

Grasping his head and turning it slightly to the side, she requested him to open his mouth. "Swallow your saliva and perk your lips like this. " She bent down and perked her lips too. "Now stick your tongue out and twirl it around mines. "

He did as she instructed. He clutched her small waist. They kissed until he got the swing of it.

"You a little quick-ass learner. You ever ate any pussy?"

Shaking his head like he was scared but he wasn't 'cause he was too excited, he squeaked out a weak no. She laid him backward on the bed and started kissing him. She kissed a trail of kisses from his lips, chest, and down to his penis. Once there she put it into her mouth. He panted like he was about to have a heart attack. His breathing was laden. His heart thumped inside his chest. If it were not for his loud gasping, he would have had to silence the loud pounding inside his chest, which felt like his heart was going to explode.

As she sucked him, she lifted her head up and said, "Boy, where you get this big dick from?"

He didn't respond because he didn't want to lose the sweet sensation flowing through his body. After he exploded in her mouth, she waited to let his heart beat return to normal. Then she stood up and lay next to him. She gently pulled him on top and clutched his butt as she kissed him and allowed him to grind into her.

"You got a big, fat dick for a young man. "

He blushed.

"I'm going to teach you how to fuck so when you start banging them young girls, you'll know exactly what to do with all this meat. "

She started kissing him as she grinded her body into him. "Can you keep a secret, Jared? I don't want you to tell anybody what I'm doing because I'm not going to jail. So promise me right now that you can you keep a secret and not tell a soul about us?"

"Yeah, I can. I promise," he said, shaking his head wildly. "I won't say a word. "

"You do and I will say you're a little liar. You know what girls think about a young man that lie on his dick?"

"No. What?"

"You a little lying fag and I know you don't want to be called that. "She grinded into him harder.

Muttering, he whispered, "No. Promise I won't ever tell. "

With that, Brenda Harris pulled his head down and kissed him so hard his toes curled. Then she grabbed his penis and entered it into her hot vagina.

Brenda was hot and horny. Having been celibate since the breakup of her marriage more than seven months earlier, she wasn't trying to hurt the boy, just wanted to feel his fullness inside her. She would teach him how to make love to a woman and he would know exactly how to make women fall for him. She felt she was also comforting the boy after losing his best friend. His dad probably never got around to telling him how to handle a woman. To Brenda, people learned faster from experience. She fucked him hard and long. "Do me from the back." She turned over and tilted her butt high in the air. He pulled her to the edge of the bed and planted himself deep inside of her.

"I'mma tear this pussy up."

Brenda laughed at his sudden cockiness. But what she didn't know was Jared had a collection of porn DVD's that he used as lessons and for his pleasure.

Jared worked Brenda over so good, she let him return to her bedroom over and over until she left and returned back to her city. She even taught him how to eat pussy. But what she gave the young Jared was experience beyond anything he could have ever imagined and for that he would be eternally grateful. Jared had skills and he had spent years honing himself as an expert lover.

Taking a puff from his cigar, he looked down at his dick and saw how hard it was. He picked up the phone and dialed Princess. She didn't answer. When the voice mail came on, he said, "Princess, if you don't call me, I'm coming over to your house." With that said, he sat the phone back into its cradle.

* * *

Princess was sitting at her desk when Jared called. She didn't feel like answering the phone so she let it go into voice mail. She played the message back and listened. "Is this dude serious? He has got to be a fool. " She banged her fists on the desk in frustration. "So all the rumors I heard about him and how cocky, smooth, and suave he is, but he's crawling around begging me like a bitch. I don't need this shit and I won't take it. "She screamed low enough for only her to hear. "That fucking pussy-whipped nigger. " She snatched the phone up and called him.

He answered on the first ring. "I want to see you tonight and that shit is final. "

"I told you this wasn't nothing but a booty call. I am not into relationships, so please stop all the drama and leave me the fuck alone. You don't want me to go and tell your girls Terri and Tameka. So you have more to lose. Just leave me alone. Punk ass!"

* * *

"This woman slammed the phone in my ear. Who in the hell does she think she is?"

Aggressively putting his cigar out, he grabbed his keys out of the middle drawer in his desk and walked out of his office. He marched through the hallway and notified his secretary that he was gone for the day. As he hit the alarm on his keypad, entered his Jag, and started the car, he wondered how he had gotten himself into this. He slapped the steering wheel. "This shit is crazy. I have to see her again, I need to feel her body wrapped around me. Never doubt this; Jared gets what the fuck he wants. " He backed out of his parking spot and zoomed out of his parking lot.

FOUR

Jared sat in the parking lot watching and waiting for Princess. He was parked next to her Lexus 450 in his Jag, a car she had never seen him in before. He didn't know what he was going to do when he saw her. He just knew that he needed to see her and taste her again. He never planned to feel like this. He loved Tameka with all his heart. He was so confused. Why did he want a woman who just wanted to have sex with him?Maybe she was doing that with other folks. Was it true what everyone had said to him about karma? So many people had said to him that what he was putting out sexing these women and leaving them hurting and broken would someday come back to haunt him. Was this it?The day his feelings would be denied?

He sat in the car drumming his fingers on the steering wheel. Bored and anxious at the same time, he rubbed his hand over and over his freshly cut fade. He opened the glove compartment and reached for a pack of gum. Removing the wrapper, he put the gum into his mouth and tossed the wrapper into a little trash bag hanging on the passenger side. While he chewed he felt a breeze come through his open window. He turned toward the breeze and noticed Princess shapely muscular legs stroll forward with swag in her step. She gripped her briefcase with her right hand when she observed a car parked close to hers. Princess fumbled with her key as she noticed the man in the car. She wanted to dash to her car but that wouldn't help; she was too close to him.

Jared bolted out of his car. "Princess, I need to talk to you now!"

"I don't have anything to say. I told you I wasn't looking for a relationship. What part of that did you not understand?"

"Come here, girl!"He extended his arms to her and pulled her into his chest. "I don't care what you said. Do you know who I am?" His eyes changed into angry slits. His forehead furrowed and his voiced boomed.

But Princess wasn't afraid. Out of all the gossip she'd heard, no one had ever accused Jared of violence. "Let me go or I will scream. "

"Scream, baby. That's how I like it. Now get into my car. "

She struggled a minute and found his grip too tight. Princess decided not to scream because this was her job and she wanted no attention brought to this crazy situation she brought on herself.

Once inside the car, Jared leaned over and kissed her. "I'm gonna tear that pussy up. "

Princess felt her panties become wet and her vagina pulsated. Damn, she wanted him too. She reached over and grabbed his head, pulling him violently into her. She kissed him and bit his lip gently.

"Mmm, I can't wait to get inside of you, baby. " Jared started the car and drove out of the parking lot. "I'll bring you back to your car later. "

* * *

While Jared had sat in the parking lot waiting, he called the Four Season Hotel and reserved the same room. Once they arrived Jared helped her out the car. "Lucky me, I got us the same room. We gonna dub this our room. This is where me and you will hang out unless you want me to buy a condo. "

"Jared, don't get beside yourself. I got what I wanted the first three times. Let me be real clear, I have a man and I love him. This is my last rump before we get married. So don't get too comfortable. "

Jared smiled. His beautiful white teeth made his eyes seem brighter as they beamed with desire. "Sure, baby, whatever you say! If your man was all that, you wouldn't have my dick in you. "

"I could say the same thing about you too. "

After registering at the front desk, they sauntered through the lobby and entered the elevator. He pulled her close and gave her a kiss that made her lift her leg and wrap it around his thigh. They kissed until the door opened with a bing.

Taking her hand, he gently caressed her breasts then he slid the key card into the door slot. Pushing the door open, he turned and picked her up like he was carrying his newlywed over the threshold. Once inside the room, he quickly eased her out of her black dress. The dress hugged her body and showed her beautiful size seven physique.

Jared removed her clothes, and slipped his finger inside her vagina. She was already wet. He used his fingers to tease and stoke her.

"Please put it in now," she begged.

There was no way he was going to put anything anywhere. It had taken a long time to get her in his arms, and there was no way he would rush into anything. With her he wanted to suck, kiss, and savor every scent on her body.

He stood behind her sucking on her neck and easing his fingers one at a time into her vagina. As she moaned and backed up to his hard dick, she began to roll her ass gently onto his hard muscle. He removed his finger and sucked her juices off. Jared used his left hand to massage her breasts. He rolled his hand in a circular motion, and then he lightly pinched them. Her nipples stood erect. Then he turned her around and put her breasts into his mouth, and he sucked on them one at a time.

"Oh damn," she continued to lament as she rubbed his head and stroked the side of his face.

Laying her back onto the bed, he lifted her clean-shaven cara-mel legs over his shoulder. He fingered her again, and when he felt the wetness nearly leaking out of her, he licked her clit, which sent her backing up and trying to get away. She was coming so hard and losing her control so much, she tried to outrun the orgasm that was so powerful. She felt if she stayed in that spot, her heart would give out from excitement.

He refused to allow her to escape the passion overflowing the room. Princess used her elbows to scoot backward; he moved in. Finally, she let out a scream and her legs shook so hard she trem-bled. Jared released them and crawled in between her thighs. He paused a second as he put on the condom. Pushing her legs open, he entered her. Kissing her, he whispered how good it felt to be inside her.

She responded, "Your dick is so good. You know how to work it, baby. "

Knowing that she was enjoying his dick, he dug deeper into her trying his best to put all of it inside. Jared beat her pussy up; they kissed and sucked on each other's lips. He pumped into her; she squeezed his butt because she wanted him to stay planted. She didn't want the feeling to leave.

"What are you doing to me?"

His movement and the rolling of his hips increased so he pumped hard into her. He kissed her neck, teased her ears with his tongue, and she rotated her hips faster. He pumped into her. They both whimpered loudly and came together. He stiffened himself and held her body tight to his. Princess gripped his penis with her muscle as tightly as she could before he slipped out.

"Hey, I don't know what it is, about you that keeps me begging. You know a brother like me don't beg for nothing. You sought me out, which truthfully I am used too, but when you started rejecting me, it set me off. I'm really digging you. Hell, girl, I can't get enough of your love. "

"I told you I was very attracted to you but I'm not interested in a relationship. Matter of fact, I have a boyfriend but I am about to let him go. My interests are in my job. I don't stay anywhere too long. So whatever attraction you think you have for me, it best for you to let it go. "

Bending down to kiss her lips, he took his tongue and circled it around inside her mouth. "That's easier said than done. After being inside of you, I want more. More time with you and I ain't having it no other way. "

Pushing him off her, she tried to rise up. "You don't run anything here. We are just fucking. Plus, don't you have a fiancée?"

Snatching her gently into him, he pulled her back underneath him and lightly planted kisses along her shoulder blade. "What does that have to do with the price of tea in China?"

Looking into his eyes to see if she could see trouble in her life, she asked him, "You're not a stalker, are you?"

"Jared doesn't stalk. He scopes out what he wants and then takes it. " He placed his hard dick inside of her pussy and started rotating in her warmth.

She quickly jumped back up.

"What do you mean by that?" Princess lifted herself up on her elbows and wrapped her legs tightly around his waist. She peered into his eyes. She wanted to be sure she could see if he was telling her the truth.

"You're on the news, right?"

"Yes, I am. " She moved to right to relieve a little pressure off her thigh from the weight of him.

Pulling her face toward him, he kissed her. "Well, think about it this way. You said you knew me from hearsay and gossip right?"

Princess pulled back from his kiss. "And?"

"I saw you probably before you ever heard my name. I've been watching you on the news for quite a long time. I've been hoping to meet you and do exactly what I'm doing to you now. I just didn't know I would want to keep seeing you. "

"Yeah, I get that, but guess what?" she asked as she gently shoved his face away.

Jared was trying hard to get another kiss in as he gently began to grind between her legs. "Open your legs, girl, and stop being stingy!"

"Don't try to ignore me. Let this be known, this is the last time you're getting between these legs, believe that my brother!"

"Yeah, okay. Mmm, it feels so good. "

"Put on a condom. "

"It feels too good to pull out now. "

"I am highly fertile. Do you want a baby by a woman not interested in a relationship with you?"

With that he pulled out and grabbed his pants and took another condom out. As he put it on, he laughed. "You certainly know how to get a man moving, don't you, sweet lady?"

"I just know you. You don't want any children who are scattered around. Now back to the subject we were discussing. This is our last time together. I am not looking for a relationship. I just wanted to sample your sex. Now I've done that, so I am through. You have totally satisfied me. "

Jared rose up on his hands and began to pound his fat and thick dick into her walls with an angry force.

79

"Oh yes, you're hitting the right spot," Princess screamed as she frantically rolled and thrusted her body back so he could go deeper inside her. "Yes, yes, fuck me hard, baby. I like it when you hit me off like this. Damn, boy, work this dick all up in me. "

He pounded her harder. It felt so damn good and he wanted to fuck her good so she would remember his dick. One thing Jared wasn't going to do was beg her to let him ride her. Hell, it was too many fish in the sea to be crying over some ass. She didn't want to see him again, that would be her damn loss. Although he enjoyed being inside her, the mere fact was he could get pussy anywhere made him harder.

He bent down and sucked her breasts. Occasionally he would lick her down her stomach, but never did he allow his penis to slip out. The feeling he was getting was so good that all he could do was gently lower his body down and grabbed her butt and tightly pull her into his penis. Sweat was running off their bodies. He slowed his rhythm and grabbed her head and pulled her toward his face. He kissed her with so much feeling, he felt a little light headed. "Damn, damn, damn. You got some good pussy, girl. How in the hell you think I'm gonna stay out of these soft-ass thighs?"

With those words, it felt as if the room had exploded but Princess didn't feel any pain, just pure pleasure as she screamed, "Jared, fuck me hard. I'm coming. I need you to fuck me like you crazy. "

And he did. With everything he had he dug deep and hit it hard. She was throwing it back at him and making all kinds of pretty faces as they both blasted and peaked at the same time. She felt the liquid she released leaking down her leg. She looked at him and tried to catch her breath as he slowly rotated his hips into her. She reached up and kissed his lips. "I'm not ready to leave. Since this is the last roll in the hay as they say, I want another round. Are you game?"

"We gonna take this to the shower. I need to taste your insides. " He lifted her off the bed and began to kiss her neck. He licked a thin line of saliva from her neck to her breasts, as he kissed and fondled her. As he grabbed her ass and lifted her up, a loud thundering at the door brought them out of their sex haze.

"Open this damn door, Princess," John shouted.

"How in the hell did he find me?Don't open the door, Jared. " Princess grabbed her clothes and worked to put them back on. Sweat beads covered her forehead; she could feel sweat dripping down her back. She searched for her shoes as Jared slipped on his slacks.

"Is that your boyfriend?He doesn't scare me. "Jared strutted to the door.

Running behind him and pleading with him not to open the door, she cried and prayed because she was terrified of what might happen.

"I'm not hiding from no one. "As Jared swung the door open in a rage, his eyes bulged when he saw his finance. "Tameka, what the hell are you doing here?"

"I've been following you and once I found out you were fucking this bitch, I contacted her boyfriend. After all, you can find out anything you want on the Internet. "

John rushed through the door and swung at Princess but his jab failed to hit her. He was so mad he was foaming at the mouth. "Who the fuck you think you are?I am gonna kick your ass. "

As he gripped her collar and tried to drag her toward him, Jared hit him from the back and knocked him off guard. As Jared thrashed John, Tameka started screaming for help.

"Somebody help!"

Princess slammed her fist into her mouth. "Bitch, this will teach your ass to mind your own damn business. "Princess continued to hit her until Jared grabbed her and told her to leave.

"Get out before the cops come and people recognize you. " He helped her get her purse and pushed her to the door. "I'll contact you later. "

"Don't waste your time. Your bitch is crazy and I'm not for this kind of drama. "

Tameka hollered, "You ain't seen drama. Wait until I fuck your ass up. "

"Like you did now? Damn, I'm scared. You little swollen bitch. "

"Go, Princess," Jared said.

As John got off the floor, Jared swung around and clocked him again, just as security entered the room.

Jared said, "Officer, this man came to my room and assaulted me. "

"He was with my woman. This motherfucker was dicking my girl."John rubbed his head.

The officers smiled. "Where is she?"

John spun around searching for Princess. "She was here. "

"Apparently she left, Officers. I am this man's fiancée, Tameka. "She pointed to Jared.

"We are going to have to further discuss that matter. " Jared spoke in a thoughtful, but condescending manner.

Tameka said, "You're not breaking off our engagement, are you?"

Jared counted to ten in his head and his jawbone throbbed. "As I said we will talk later, but right now, get your ass out of here. "

Tameka was pissed. Her eyes seemed to cast off a dark hooded look. Her irises looked suddenly gray. Her peanut-colored skin tone darkened like a shade had been pulled over her head. Her face had a layer of sheen and a small puddle of sweat in the middle of her forehead. She was angry and ready to become argumentative but Jared was not having it. He was pissed that Tameka had the audacity to follow him and then to put him and Princess in harm's way by bringing an adversary to him. She had no idea if he would be packing a gun and had intentions on shooting. She simply risked their lives. He wasn't sure if he would ever trust her again.

"Are you pressing charges against this guy?"One of the officers wanted to know. "If you are, we can take him in now. "

"Nah!I'm not pressing charges but if anything happens to Princess Mays, Officer, you know he did it. "

The officer raised a brow. "Princess Mays, the reporter?"

"Yes, Officer. This fool took a couple of swings at her, and I want him to know that if he so much as touches her, I am personally gonna clock his ass. "

"My advice to you is to call us if you have any more trouble with him and let us do our job. "The officer turned to John and with a stern voice and the point of a finger said, "Don't let us see you anymore. And if you so much as touch Princess Mays, consider your life over. Got that?"

"None of y'all got to worry about me touching her. As far as I'm concerned, that tramp is not worth my time. "

"John Boy!" Jared stared so hard; the only thing moving on his face was an angry tick jumping in his cheek.

"Nigger, I got you damn John Boy!Fuck with me and see. "

"You ain't worth my time. What did you say you did professionally?"

"Fuck you!" John decided to bounce to prevent another altercation. "I'm not going to fight over no whores, and you can believe that!"

Before Jared could say another word, John dashed out of the suite. "Officer, everything seems to be fine. "

"Jared, man," the officer said and gave him a pound, "Be careful, man. You can get yourself into a lot of mess over women. "

"Nah, brother, I don't roll like that!I am a lover, not a fighter; but if I have to I will whup some ass. "

The second officer asked, "You sure Princess Mays is fine?"

"Yeah, man, I wouldn't let anything happen to her. "

"Since no one wanted to press charges and no damage has been done to the room, I guess we're not needed. You got some ironing out to do with the two ladies. "The officer extended his hand and shook Jared's. "Well, take care. "

They walked out the room and Jared walked over to the table and picked up his cell phone and called Princess. "Are you okay?"

Speaking through pursed lips to express her resentment to Jared and to show him that he was getting on her last nerve, she asked, "Why?"

"I was worried about you. Where are you so I can come get you?"

"I'm in my skin, and this time you won't be jumping in. For your information I am minding my own damn business, so I suggest you make this your last call to me. I'm through with you. "

As Jared button his pants and put on his belt, he heard nothing but the sound of dead air.

FIVE

Nothing pissed Jared off as much as a woman getting into his business and causing trouble. His first visit was to Tameka. He wanted her to know that for now the engagement was off. He'd explained to her why. He pounded on her door with both fists so hard, the front window shook and threatened to shatter into little pieces. Tameka opened the door and Jared charged in.

"You are not my wife, Tameka, and until you are, you have nothing to do with who I sleep with. I don't know what part of that you don't understand. "

Slamming the door hard, she shrieked, "What in the hell do you mean?"

"Just what I said. Do you see a ring on my damn finger?" Jared grabbed his ring finger and held it up to her face. He tightened his lips together and talked through his teeth, "Do you see a ring?"

With his finger dead in her face, she huffed and puffed and stared at his finger. She even snapped at it as if she would bite it off, but settled down enough to say, "You asked me to be your wife and that meant— to me— that your running around in the street was over. "

Leaning back against the front door and shoving his left hand into his pocket, Jared pressed his finger to his right temple and rubbed it as if he was having one bad headache. "Sweetheart, apparently there is a misunderstanding, considering we have never discussed this. Until you walked down the aisle with me and we say I do, this is my damn dick. I do what the hell I please with it. Now if you can't handle that, then you know what you can do. "

Screaming and pointing her finger at Jared, Tameka wiped the tears that rained down her face. "I can't believe that you expect me to accept you are going to have sex with other women until we are married. What in the hell kind of sense does that make?"

Jared turned to leave. "You think about that; and if you can't find an answer, you know this engagement is off. If you decide that you can handle me still being a man until the wedding date when I will give everything up, then call me. But, baby, you know I love you, but today you could have brought harm to me and an innocent person. What if that nigger had brought a gun to that hotel?Then what?What if he shot and killed us both?Then who would you be with?You know the more I think about this the angrier I become. As a matter fact, since your ass was so nosey and was following me and getting all up in my business, consider this engagement off. "

He walked briskly to the door. Tameka was so close to his heels he felt her step on the back of his Ferragamos.

"Please, baby, I am so sorry. Please don't leave like this. I love you so much, that's why I did what I did. I'm sorry, you can do what you want until our wedding day, and then your sleeping with other women will be a thing of the past. I just love you. "She wiped her hand across her tear drenched face.

"We'll see. A trust bond was broken. How do I know you'll never step like that again into my business?"He poked his chest out because he was the man.

"It won't happen again. I promise. "She grabbed his face between her hands and kissed his lips. "Please forgive me, baby. "

"I forgive you but the violation of our trust I won't forget. " Jared walked out and slammed the door. He left Tameka standing there crying.

SIX

Jared leaned against his car and raked a hand across his head. He was pissed. He paced a few steps from the driver's side of his car and suddenly found himself walking up to the front end and then again to the back. Why was he tripping about these women? He'd never been in a situation like this, and the worst part was he was feeling Princess. Even though he had been watching her on television daily for the past year or more while envisioning how it would feel to fuck her, he never dreamed he would be tripping over wanting to see her again. Damn, he was the brother who was clear about what he wanted from a lady and had never had a problem with sexing one until she begged him to stop. Then, just as suddenly as it started, it was over. But there was something so familiar, so comfortable with Princess. He just didn't understand. But he wanted to see her again. He paced back and forth on a straight dirt path that once grew grass alongside his car and decided to go to get a drink. Damn, he needed to think. He was fucked up.

He pressed the keypad and unlocked his car. He eased onto the leather seat and started the car. As the car started, he wiped the sweat that soaked his forehead. Then he looked into his rearview and through his side view mirrors and pulled out into traffic. After having a drink, his head would be clear as to what his next steps would be.

* * *

Jared arrived at The Broadway in Florissant. He wanted to stay as close to Princess as he could. It took him about forty minutes to get to the club. He strolled in, greeted several men he had seen before, and proceeded to walk to the bar. He ordered some gin and orange juice and a beer. The atmosphere provided him with the comforts he needed:the low level lighting, the ability to be incognito, and the privacy to think. He relaxed on the barstool and sniffed the smoke floating through the air. He needed one of his cigars.

As he pondered his feelings, he couldn't understand the hold Princess had on him. It felt like she had taken a pair of vice grips and tightened them around his heart. He was baffled about his feelings. Never had he allowed someone to control his feelings, and this simply didn't feel right. Being from a two-parent home where opportunities to be and do whatever you wanted were plentiful, he was accustomed to getting what he wanted. He was wealthy. His father's death had left him and his mom financially free. Life for Jared had provided him with never-ending choices and plenty of sexual prospects. He didn't have to beg for anything or ask twice and yet here he was begging. That didn't sit too well with him.

He slammed his shot glass down on the bar's counter, looked into the smoked streaked mirror directly in front of him, and stared at the wine glasses hanging from the rafter of the low ceiling. He grabbed a handful of the fresh peanuts that the bartender placed in front of him and tossed them into his mouth—his cockiness was back. That self-confident player who owned his own playground of fun was back. Never would he allow himself to bask in the pain of rejection.

He laid down a fifty on the counter. "Thanks man!"

The bartender reached over and they gave each other a fist-to-fist pound.

Today was the last day he would beg a woman to be with him. He leaped off the leather barstool and strutted out of the lounge to find Princess.

* * *

Jared knocked on the door of Princess's condo. It was six hours after the hotel dilemma. Nearly 9:00 PM, he was tired, confused, and ready to call a truce with Princess. He wasn't sure what he would say or do but he knew he needed to clear the air.

As he knocked on the door, the front window curtain swung back. Then the door opened. Jared's mouth dropped wide open. He couldn't believe it. He hadn't seen her since he was a fifteen-year-old, nineteen years to be exact. He always wondered where she had gone. He asked his mother a couple of times where she was but never got an answer. He had missed her kisses and the sweet taste of her pussy. Now, here she stood looking as beautiful as ever. She had to be about forty-nine, but she looks about the same as she did when he last saw her.

"Brenda Harris!"

"Jared, is that you, boy?"She reached out and pulled him to her.

He clutched her around the waist and kissed her cheek. As he did so, he observed Princess staring directly at him.

"How did you find me?"Brenda was excited. "How is your

mom?Is she okay? Does she still live here in St. Louis?"She twirled him around. "You have grown into a very handsome man. It's so good to see you. "

Jared couldn't breathe. It felt like he did fifteen years ago laying on his back while Brenda rode on his dick. He still felt his heart beating fast and he remembered her sexy smelling scent. He inhaled her flowery fragrance. He just stood there smiling like a fool.

EPILOGUE

After Brenda invited Jared into the house and introductions were made, Jared discovered that Princess Mays was Brenda's only child. Princess never used her last name, which was Harris. She used her mother's maiden name.

After much discussion Jared found out that his mother, Gwen, had found out about their sexual escapades and had banned Brenda from her home and life. Gwen wanted to press charges against Brenda, her best friend, for statutory rape, but eventually decided against it on the condition that Brenda just disappeared.

Brenda remarried Princess's father after they attended counseling and reconciled their differences. When Brenda was visiting Gwen, Princess, who was thirteen at the time, was staying with her grandmother attending school. Brenda didn't want to remove Princess from school while she stayed with Gwen during that time. She confessed to Jared that she too was suffering from depression due to her husband's cheating. Never would she have done what she had if she was in her right mind.

Brenda apologized to Jared for everything while he thanked her for his skills. When she asked why he arrived to her daughter's house that day, he admitted they'd briefly dated and he was coming to let her know that he was going to remain with his fiancée. While they talked, Princess had left the room only to return when they had changed the topic. So she never knew about her mother and Jared's love affair, only that their mothers were once best friends.

Jared and Princess never got back together because he believed there was too much history with her mother, and he would never come between a mother and her daughter. He was a lover, not a manipulator who would destroy a parent and child relationship.

He and Tameka made up, and although they weren't planning on getting married, Jared was still the pretty boy player who had a reputation for loving as many women as possible while showing them one heck of a sexy good time.

THE SECRET

By Cecelia Edwards

ONE

I found a narrow path between my moving boxes to get to my ringing phone.

"Hey girl, how you doing?"My girl Theresa said when I answered the phone.

"I'm… I'm fine, I guess. I mean, how else should I feel after something like this?"I looked around at all the unpacked boxes scattered throughout the house, still not believing how things turned out.

"Yeah, I know, this must be hard for you to deal with. "

"It is. I mean, no one gets married expecting to get divorced. "

"I know. "

"You pretty much go in thinking:This is the person I'm going to be with for the rest of my life. Then, to fail with your marriage—"

"Girl, don't feel bad, fifty percent of marriages end up in divorce. So your situation isn't new. "

"I know, but—" I looked around at my new house, filled with boxes and the realization that now I was alone in life. "—knowing that doesn't make me feel better. I wanted my marriage to last. "

"Christy, everybody does, but its okay. Look, I'm coming down there and we're gonna celebrate your new single status with style!"

I rolled my eyes and sighed. "Okay, as long as you say so," I said, dragging my finger across the top of one of my boxes.

Theresa laughed. "Not only do I say so, but I know so. Remember, I should be arriving at the train station at 4:50 Friday afternoon. Make sure you're there to pick me up. "

"Now, have I ever left you stranded?"

"Christy, don't try to play me. You remember that one time you overslept when you were supposed to pick me up from the airport?"

"I know, I know… but that was in college! I didn't realize how tiring Econ would have been as a major. I once overslept a final!But now, since I haven't been studying all night, I should be able to pick you up on time. "

"Thank you kindly, Hun. "

"All right. Well, girl, I need to finish unpacking. So I'll see you on Friday. "

"All righty, and hey, call me if you need to talk some more, okay?"

"I definitely will. Love ya, Hun. "

"Love you too. "

I placed my cell phone down on top of a box labeled "Kitchen" and looked around at my new domicile. "Not too bad," I whispered to myself as I walked from room to room in my two-bedroom house. Even with carpeted floors, my steps seemed to echo as I walked down the hallway to each room. I didn't need a lot of space because it was only me. But after signing the leasing agreement, having the cable and Internet installed, and after my family members left from helping me move in, the house began to seem humongous. As beautiful as it was, and as excited as I was to start this new chapter in my life, I was also reminded of the life I left.

A single act of honesty is what brought Reginald and me together. While going inside to pay for my gas at a gas station, he was walking out, and putting his wallet back in his back pocket. While doing so, some money fell out that he didn't see. I picked it up and chased after him to give it back to him.

"Hey, you dropped this twenty," I had said.

He looked at me incredulously. "Are you sure it's mine?"He said, grabbing his wallet and looking inside of it to make sure.

"Do you think that I would just hand a random stranger a twenty-dollar bill?"I was beginning to get annoyed. The cold air hit me in the face and I tightened the scarf around my neck. All I wanted to do was to give his money back, go ahead and pay for my gas, and leave.

He picked up on my agitation and apologized. "It's just that… you don't find a lot of honest people nowadays. "

"It's no big deal," I said as I thrust the money into his hand and quickly walked into the gas station. I was just getting over a cold, and I didn't want to get sick again. There was just only so many days I could miss being an accountant for the finance firm I worked for. As I paid for my gas, I could feel him watching me, but by the time I got out, he had left.

About a week later I went to the same gas station and he was there, as if he had been waiting for me. I attempted to just walk past him but he stopped me.

"Excuse me, I never really do this, but I was wondering if I could talk to you for a minute. "

After a long day of work I didn't have any interest in talking. All I wanted to do was crash in front of my television, but there was something so genuine about his request that I granted it. As we stood in the lit area by the pumps, he told me about how ever since I gave him his money back he couldn't stop thinking about the honest but modest girl who'd crossed his path. Every day that he got off of work he would come and wait until around the time he last saw me, hoping I would reappear. He asked if he could pay me back, and I suggested that we meet at a coffee shop down the street that Saturday.

Saturday came and we talked and got to know each other. I didn't give him my phone number until about two months after we met each other at the coffee shop. Finally, after about three months we went on our first official date at an Italian restaurant. Ten months after that we went to the courthouse and got married.

Three months into our marriage, we began to realize that we were good on paper but did not mesh well together. Our love life was amazing, and even now, sometimes, I could feel his hands graze over my body, and I could feel his lips on my neck and feel them trail down my body as he headed down to find the sweet spot between my legs. As I began to yearn to feel for him again, I had to physically shake the memory out of my mind.

Not wanting to think too hard about my failed marriage, I decided that productivity was the only way to get my mind off of Reginald, so I began to unpack.

After about six hours, the house was as unpacked as it was going to get. My bedroom, living room, and kitchen were set up nicely. The second bedroom was just going to have to be a safe haven for the other boxes that I would eventually unpack. I sat down on my living room couch, turned on the TV, and found a movie to watch. "Oh cable, you'll never leave me. "

Not really paying attention to my movie, I ordered Chinese food. Once it got there, I lay back down on the couch and looked out my windows at the trees and orange sky, while another movie played on my TV.

I'm an emotional eater. And while married to my husband, I would eat to compensate for being lonely; the only company I had was the knowledge of gaining forty-five pounds. During my divorce, my mother persuaded me to start working out to stave off depression; doing so I lost fifty pounds. Resolved not to gain it back, I put my leftovers in my refrigerator and decided to watch movies in my bedroom.

As I lay down and watched a mafia movie, I caressed my stomach. Trying my best to forget about my past life, I took a nap.

After waking up, I decided to splurge on a Pay-Per-View movie. Going to the menu, I began to search through the categories. The "Adult" section seemed to illuminate much more brightly to me than the other categories. I never thought about paying to watch adult movies, but for some reason I began to feel sort of exhilarated. I took a shower, walked into the bedroom, shut the door, grabbed my vibrator, and searched through the subcategories in the "Adult" collection. The summaries of the movies painted pictures of men with women, women with women, toys participating in the pleasure, and anything that could appeal to anyone's sexual appetite. A title of one film caught my eye and the summary immediately made me excited. Once on, I watched and waited until I got fully turned on then I guided my vibrator to my clit.

The woman in the video, a thick redbone, guided her hands to a petite woman's breast, grabbed it, and then gently, but eagerly brought the nipple to her mouth. The redbone's sucking technique seemed so divine, I could feel myself becoming turned on between my legs. The light exposed the women's smooth skin in great detail. The redbone slowly took the nipple out of her mouth and guided herself south, opened Petite's legs, licked her moist slit.

I turned my vibrator on and put it against my hot button of desire as Redbone licked, teased, and sucked Petite's pussy. I looked on as a blonde woman joined in. Petite was eating Blondie's pussy while Blondie had her hand in Redbone's panties, fingering her. As Redbone was being fingered, she squeezed Blondie's breasts together. My body began to undulate with enjoyment as the vibrator continued to deliver pleasure to my sopping wet pussy. My eyes were glued to the screen as Petite rearranged herself to sit Redbone's face. As Redbone ate the Petite's pussy, she simultaneously played with Petite's large breasts. As her nipples were being twisted, she bounced with pleasure on Redbone's mouth that was happy to taste her.

"Oh my God, yes. Eat her pussy," I said with a moan as I continued to keep the vibrator pressed against my vagina and grabbed one of my own breasts with my free hand. After about fifteen minutes, I was brought to pleasure by my vibrator and a scene with Redbone and Petite grinding their pussies together while Blondie sat outside the action taking turns sucking on their nipples.

As the warmth began to leave my body and my temperature was brought back to normal, I began to feel feelings of condemnation and doubt. What am I doing? Am I a lesbian? Why did I just masturbate to lesbian porn?

I never had the urge to masturbate to pornography before, but stumbling upon lesbian porn drew me in like a moth to a flame.

I grabbed my laptop and looked online to see if masturbating to lesbian pornography was an indicator of sexual preference, but I found other women who admitted that just because they enjoyed masturbating to it, didn't mean that they preferred women. I couldn't believe that I was beginning to question my sexual orientation, but I had to remind myself that I never found women attractive in real life and that I had a very satisfying sexual relationship with my husband while we were together.

However, while watching that movie, I found myself envying the women in the movie, and I even daydreamed of joining in. I was shocked to find myself muttering to the television about how beautiful the women's breasts were and how I wish I could be there to suck on their nipples.

My mind put me in the movie as the star. I opened up Petite's legs and buried my tongue in her vagina, enjoying every second of it. Redbone grinded my pussy as she grabbed my breasts in desire. The movie in my mind encompassed us women nestling our tongues between the folds of one another's vagina, sucking on one another's breasts, doing the 69 position, using toys on one another, or grinding our pussies together.

As I watched each scene, my vagina craved attention. Without realizing it, my hand wandered down to my own pussy and I started playing with it even after using my vibrator, masturbating to the beautiful women who chose to pleasure women who were just as beautiful.

As these thoughts began to emerge after enjoying my solo session, I tried to physically shake it out of my head. When that didn't work, I turned my TV to another mafia movie and fell asleep.

* * *

"You didn't forget!"

"Not only did I not forget, I'm actually early. "I smiled at Theresa while she put her seatbelt on. After it securely clicked, she reached over and gave me a hug.

"Wow!Look at you, you look so good!"

"Thanks, girl, nothing says getting over a failed marriage like fitting in your favorite pair of jeans. "

"Nope!"

I looked at Theresa confused. "What are you nope-ing for?"

"This is not a let's-feel-bad-about-the-divorce weekend. This is a celebrate-Christy's-freedom weekend!Therefore, nothing self-deprecating, no self-pity, no—"

I laughed and smiled at Theresa, "All right, all right. I get it. So, what is on the agenda?"

"First, I need to pick something up at that grocery store. You know the one with the funny name. I ordered something to mark the beginning of our celebration, then a liquor store, and finally your house. "

"Apparently we're going to vomit during this weekend," I joked while driving to the store.

"Only if we're lucky," Theresa joked as I turned to go down Jefferson Street.

* * *

I fumbled with the keys as I held Theresa's luggage in one hand and a bag of alcohol in the other.

"Christy, I told you not to carry my bag. This is your weekend. "

"Theresa, no matter whose weekend it is, I'm gonna be a proper hostess. So, grab the keys out of my hand and open up my door. "

Theresa did so, and we both walked into my new house.

"Wow… Christy, this is a lot nicer than you described it," Theresa said as her eyes traveled around the kitchen.

"Thanks, I built it myself," I joked as I placed everything down on the table.

At the grocery store Theresa made me wait in the car while she picked up what she ordered. She bounced back with a white box labeled "pastry" and wouldn't tell me what was in it. After I placed everything down I immediately headed to the box.

Jokingly slapping my hand, Theresa stopped me. "No!No peek-ies!This is for tomorrow and it's a surprise. Plus, you have to start getting ready. "

My face immediately dropped. I was not interested in going anywhere, especially knowing that I might have to run into someone I knew and explain why my husband wasn't with me. "Theresa—"

"Christy, didn't I say that this weekend is going to be a celebration?Now, I leave on Sunday. That only gives us a night and a day of celebrating your freedom, so let's take advantage of it. Now, let me see that beautiful smile. "She teased as she nudged me.

Begrudgingly I allowed a smile to spread across my lips.

"There you go. Now, get in the shower while I put this stuff up. When I'm done, I'll pick out your clothes, okay?"

"Wait, I don't even get to pick out what I'm wearing?"

"No!Oh, and whatever I pick out, you have to wear it, okay?"

"Reesey, you know I hate surprises. "

"But you love me, right?"

"Of course. "

"So get your ass in the shower. Oh!Curl your hair with the curling iron!You're gonna look fierce, girl!"

I walked to my room and got naked. I stopped and admired my newly shaped body in my bedroom mirror. With all of the frustrations of moving into a new place, I never got a chance to take a full view of how my body looked without the extra padding. Facing the mirror, I admired how my breasts seemed perkier from losing the weight. My stomach had slight lines of precision, but no six-pack how I liked it and my love handles were gone. My thighs were still thick, but the look of cottage cheese permeating under my skin no longer existed. My thighs no longer touched when I walked, and my vagina looked fresh and clean from my weekly wax. I turned to my profile and looked as my butt stuck out—draped with taut chocolate skin—and how my stomach was no longer sticking out past my breasts. Then, suddenly my door flew open.

"Oh my goodness! Theresa, you scared me. "

"Christy… why are you not in the shower yet? No dilly-dally-ing. We have a schedule to keep. Now get that naked body in the shower. "

I sighed. "All right. Let me just toss my clothes in the dirty clothes hamper in the laundry room. "I bounced to the hamper across the hall, all the while feeling her eyes watching me. Theresa and I had been friends for about four years now, ever since we lived in the same dorm, but on different floors during our freshman year of college. We've never seen each other naked, though. So I knew her watching was more so out of surprise with my bodi-ly freedom. Even when we went to the gym to take a break from me studying economics and accounting and her Poli Sci class, we always showered whenever we got back to our dorms. However, I've always been a little too comfortable in my own skin, and have always been known with my ex-husband to walk around naked for hours after a shower. That's why I always had a single dorm room in college.

I went back to my room and before I got in the shower, Theresa stopped me.

She said, "Girl, I just have to let you know, I know that you were working out during the divorce, but your body looks amazing. Congrats, girl. "

I blushed. "Thank you. Yours do too. "

Theresa laughed and put her hand to her flat stomach. "Thanks, but I'm just trying to be like you, girl. Now, get in that shower. Remember, curl your hair!"

I got in the shower feeling happy, confident, and invigorated to go out that night. It felt good to know that just because I went through such a stressful situation that doing something to bring self-improvement would benefit me physically and emotionally.

After showering, moisturizing, and curling my naturally long hair, I walked out of my bathroom to find a purple cutoff sweater, a red pair of acid washed skinny jeans, and some high-top sneakers. To the right I saw a long necklace and some doorknocker hoop earrings. "Theresa! What in the world?"

"Hey, no questions yet," she said while I admired her newly crimped short hairstyle. "Now I'm about to shower and get ready. When I come out, I'm expecting to see you fully dressed, and have some makeup on. "

I did what was expected of me. When Theresa stepped out of the bathroom, she was fully dressed and had applied her makeup in the bathroom. She had a pink top that hugged her light complexioned frame and a netted top that draped off her shoulders. She tied a matching pink ribbon in her crimped hair. Her legs were highlighted in a tight, lime green miniskirt and a white belt that slung off of her hips. She twirled around, showing me the finished

110

product. Her cross earrings and cross necklace swung, and with her cutoff, lace gloved hands, she smoothed her outfit down, fingertips lingering on her bare midriff. We burst out laughing and began jumping up and down while complimenting each other.

"Oh my goodness, Christy! That outfit looks good on you!"

"You look great too, Theresa. Oh my God, I am so excited, and slightly nervous. "

"Don't worry; I'll take good care of you. Now, let's go to the Calendar Club. "

We bounced to the car, giddy and laughing, and made our way to the club. When we arrived, we saw the line was full of people dressed in '80's attire. Smiling at Theresa, I parked. "Oh my goodness, how did you pick this out?"

"It's amazing where Internet research will lead you. Now, are you ready?"

"Hell yeah!" We both jumped out of the car and headed toward the line. The music blasted and we could hear it in line. With each echoing beat my anticipation grew. When it was our turn, we entered the club and were swept back into the '80s. From wall to wall the club was full of people dancing and enjoying the whimsy. We both walked over to the bar—resolved to only have one drink that night—and ordered two shots of tequila. Holding our shot glasses toward each other, Theresa leaned toward me and yelled in my ear, "This is for necessary exits, new beginnings, and looking hot!"

"Cheers!" I yelled, and then we licked salt off of our hands, took the shot, and then sucked on a lime. I squinted my face up as the shot went down my throat. I hadn't drunk alcohol since college, so it was as if taking my first drinks again. "Whoa!"I yelled as I slammed my glass down on the bar. Theresa's face was twisted as well. I laughed until it returned to its normal appearance.

"You make that shot look really good," I heard a baritone voice whisper in my ear. I turned to see a tall, dark complexioned guy smile at me.

His head was shaved, and he had on a pink suit with a green tank top underneath. His smile was beautiful as he flashed a straight set of teeth in my direction. I smiled back.

I said, "It's because it was good. "

"May I buy you another?"

At the mention of that, my heart began to sink as I remembered the awkwardness of flirting and dating and how I thought that I would never have to endure it again. "What's your name?"

"Lawrence," he said, leaning against the bar with his body facing me.

"Lawrence, thank you so much, but I have to decline. Thank you, but—" I gestured toward Theresa who was looking at him as well, smiling. "—this is a girls' night out. "

Still smiling, he said, "No problem. Let me know if you change your mind. "

I touched his arm. "I definitely will. "

Then he walked away.

"Christy!That guy was hot. Why didn't you talk to him?"

"Girl, that's the last thing I need. "

Theresa's eyes went northward as she thought for a second. "Yeah, you're right. Now, let's dance the night away!"She grabbed my hand and led me to the dance floor. There, we both danced facing each other and politely dismissing men who wanted to dance with us. This was going to be an all-girls' night, and we were there for fun, not for flirting.

At about two, we decided to leave and head back to my place. My sweater had a coating of sweat on the inside; it felt awkward to have it against my skin. The entire time in the car we laughed and talked about how much fun the night was.

"You know, I hadn't really been out when I was married. "

Theresa raised a brow and turned toward me. "Why not?"

"Reginald hated going out, so I was in the house all the time. "

"Well. " Theresa put her hand on my thigh as I was pulling up in my driveway. "I'm glad I was able to give you a taste of what the outside world was like. Was it anything like you remembered?"She joked.

I laughed and looked at her as we pulled into my garage. "Even better. "

* * *

"I think I'm going to shower before bed. I'm a little too sweaty for my liking," I said as I walked to my bedroom.

Theresa followed me into my room. Once inside, she took her

shoes off and placed them beside my door. "Me too, I'll jump in after you," she said as she walked over to my dresser and looked at her reflection in the mirror.

"Make yourself comfortable and I'll be out in a minute," I said as I pulled the sweater over my head.

"Christy!"Theresa's eyes widened. "When did you get so buxom?"

"What are you talking about?"I was confused.

"Girl, when did your titties get so big?"

I couldn't help but laugh. "Oh!Girl, they're not that big. If you wanted to see some big boobies, you should have seen me with that extra weight. These balloons were huge. "

Theresa laughed and then pulled her shirt off, exposing her black bra. "I wish mine were bigger. "

"Girl, your breasts are good!You know, when I was younger I used to pray that I would have big titties. Now that I have them... yeah, I could do without. "I laughed and gently slapped her on the back.

"Girl, you better use those titties. If I were you, I would be like hey boys," she said as she pushed her breasts together, leaned over, and shook them at her reflection.

I laughed as she stood next to me. I bent down and took my pants off and saw her still gripping her breasts together. "Theresa. "I playfully slapped her hands from her breasts. "Instead of feeling yourself up, decide where you would like to sleep?In bed with me or on the couch?I was too lazy to set your room up. "

She plopped down on my bed. "Here is fine. Go ahead and shower so I can keep on checking myself out," she joked, putting her shirt back on.

I stepped into my bathroom, took off my bra and panties, and stepped into my shower. As I turned the water on, Theresa came in.

She said, "Hey, can I ask you something?"

"Sure!"I yelled over the sound of the water hitting my body. Through the Plexiglas sliding door, I could see her silhouette glide to the toilet and sit on the lid.

"How are you really doing?You know, with all of this?"

I thought as I lathered the soap on my washcloth and began to rub it over my skin. "You know, the transition is hard, but it gets better every day. "I then opened the door slightly, and stuck my head out. "Especially with friends like you!"

Theresa smiled at me. "It's nothing, Hun. As long as I can be there for you. Now hurry up before I jump in there with you," she joked.

"All right, let me rinse. "I turned around in the shower, making sure that the water hit everywhere the soap was.

"Oh la la!Shake that body, girl!"Theresa yelled at me.

I laughed, bent over, and shook my butt toward her.

"Woo-hoo!"She said.

I turned off the water and stepped out of the shower. My towel was next to Theresa's head. "All right. It's all yours. "I smiled at Theresa as I grabbed my towel and began to dry my naked body.

"Thanks," she said as she stripped down in front of me and stepped into the shower.

I grabbed my lotion and began to moisturize my body. "Hey, Reesey thanks again for tonight and for coming here this weekend. I really appreciate it. "

"No problem. Thanks for letting me take you to a random '80's dance party. Tomorrow will be a lot more chiller. Just the two of us eating great food, drinking, and watching your favorite movies. "

I smiled. I hadn't had a chance to really sit back with a friend and relax since the divorce. "Thanks again. "

"No problem. Hey, you want to fall asleep to a movie?"

"Of course!"

"Okay, you pick one and I'll be right out. "

I bounced to my bedroom, put on a pair of panties and a T-shirt, and grabbed a few selections. Opening my TV cabinet, which housed my flat screen, I could see Theresa coming up behind me naked. "Let me see what movies you have. "I gave her my three selections, thinking about how free Theresa had been since she'd been at my house. "How about that one?" she said, pointing to one of my favorites.

"Sounds like a plan," I said.

She walked to her bag, opened it, grabbed a pair of underwear and a T-shirt, and put them on.

She climbed in my queen-sized bed as I turn off the light. Putting the movie in, the room was illuminated by the television's screen. I walked to the right side of the bed and slipped in under the covers. "Good night, Reesey. Thanks again for coming. "

"No problem, Christy, and if you liked tonight, you're gonna love tomorrow. "

* * *

At around noon I awakened to the sounds of someone cooking in my kitchen. For a slight moment I panicked. I had only been in my house for about a week or so, and wasn't prepared to be burglarized. Right when I was about to hide under the bed, I saw Theresa's bag and remembered everything.

I walked toward the kitchen and the smell of eggs, toast, and bacon got stronger with each step. "Good morning, Chef!"

"I think you mean good afternoon. It's 12:30. "

"Wow… I didn't realize I slept that long. "

"Well, you hadn't busted a move in a long time," she joked as she took the skillet with the eggs off the eye that was cooking them. I went and sat down at a chair at my table. On my plate toast and bacon was already placed, and once I sat down, Theresa used the spatula to slide eggs unto my plate. She then put some on hers and she sat down opposite from me.

"Did you sleep well?"I said.

"Of course. But, I slept like a log. What about you?"

Chewing from the bite I took from my toast, egg, and bacon sandwich, I answered covering my mouth, "Pretty good. Excited about having a mellow day. "

"And that you shall, darling. That you shall. Let's say we start the festivities around two o'clock. I'm gonna shower after this. "

"I'll get in after you. "

"Great. "She took a sip from a glass by her plate. "Put on some cute pajamas when you get out of the shower. "

"You're the boss," I said, laughing. I picked up my empty plate, put it in my dishwasher, and went back to my room and lay down. "I'm going to nap until you get out of the shower. Can you wake me up close to one thirty?"

"Surely can," she yelled back cheerfully.

I smiled as I closed my eyes, preparing to fall back asleep.

* * *

With a pair of gray knee-length basketball shorts with my college's emblem on it and a matching top, I walked into my living and was surprised. Aqua, purple, green, and yellow streamers were hanging from wall to wall, and a banner that read:"FREEDOM" accompanied a ball and chain going through it, hung in the door way. On the coffee table was a one layered circular vanilla frosted cake that had a woman in a ripped wedding dress kicking at her groom.

I heard Theresa's footsteps coming up behind me, and I turned to see her in a pair of pink pajama shorts and a tight fitting top. "Hey!Happy Freedom Day!" she said while raising a bottle of Jack Daniels in her right hand and champagne in her left.

"Oh my goodness, this is fantastic!Thank you, Reesey. "

"No problem," she said as she walked past me and placed the

champagne in a bowl of ice and the Jack next to the cake. "Now, I ordered your favorite pizza while you were in the shower and it should be here really soon. I also bought some nacho stuff in the store yesterday when I picked up your cake, in case you want that instead. Oh, and there's ice cream in the freezer. I'm thinking tonight we'll have—"

The doorbell interrupted her.

She grabbed her wallet and headed toward the door while still talking:"Kahlua and ice cream floats, just to make sure… keep the change… no problem… we getting real nice and toasted tonight. "She walked back with two large pizzas and a two liter of strawberry soda.

"Wow… this is fantastic. Thank you. "

"Now—" She plopped down on the couch and looked up at me. "Are you ready?"

"Yes!"I emphatically yelled, sitting down right next to her. She smiled and handed me a Princess Tiara, and she turned a movie on.

Halfway into the second movie, two slices of the second pizza was being digested, half of the bottle of champagne had been drunk, and I laid on the couch with my calves resting on the armrest. Theresa was leaning on the armrest on her side.

"Theresa, this really has been a great weekend so far. Thank you so much. "

"No problem, doll," Theresa said, smiling at me.

"I still can't believe we went to an '80's party last night. That's the last thing I would have expected, but it was so fun!"

"I actually still can't believe you turned that sexy chocolate man down. "

I laughed while my mind went back to him. His face flashed in my mind and my smile lingered. "Yeah, he was sexy as hell, huh?But I can't do that anymore. "

Theresa shifted her body to face me. "You mean, you're not ready to date again?"

"Nope, I mean date ever again. I don't want to date. I don't want to get in a relationship, none of it, ever again. "

"Okay, no more champagne for you," she said jokingly, moving the bottle away from me.

I sat up, shifted my body toward her, and explained:"No, I'm serious. I'm done with relationships. "

"So, you're just not going to date anymore?Is that what you're telling me?"

"Yep," I said proudly, taking a sip from my champagne flute.

She sat back against the couch armrest, still facing me. "What are you going to do for sex?"

Looking her plainly in the face as she took a sip from her own champagne flute, I said, "Masturbate. "

At that answer, she started choking on her champagne. She placed her flute down so she wouldn't drop it. She looked at me as she kept on coughing, struggling to get out what she wanted to say.

After clearing her throat, she laughed. "You seem just too goody to do something like that. Do you even know how?"

I picked a pillow from the floor and tossed it at her. "Yes!Com'on, I'm not that good. "

Her eye began to twinkle.

"Really?What do you do?"She sat up and was all ears.

"Well," I said, before I downed the rest of the champagne in my flute. I knew I was going to need to be a little more than tipsy to continue having this conversation. I've never told anyone these things about me. Theresa and I had been pretty good friends in college, and she's proven to be so amazing since my divorce. She'd never been judgmental and I felt that if I could trust anyone, I could trust her. "I put on some porn. "

"Whoa, Whoa, Whoa!You watch porn?"She said, her eyes bulging behind this new information on me.

"Oh my goodness. Yes, Reesey!Why are you acting so shocked?"I said.

"Because. I just could never picture you doing something like that. You just seem so pristine. I never thought that I would hear those words coming out of your mouth. "

"Well, they are," I said sarcastically.

"Hold that thought," she said, getting up and pulling at the bottom of her shorts to release them from being gathered at her crotch. "I might need something stronger to drink than this to handle finding out that my sweet lil' Christy is a naughty girl. "She teased. She ran into the kitchen, brought back the bottle of Jack, the two liter of strawberry soda, and two glasses. She mixed the two drinks in our glasses and handed me one. We clinked our glasses together and took a large gulp. After her gulp, she placed her glass back on the table and turned to me. "Now, tell me about your alleged porn fascination. "

"Well. " I giggled, starting to feel the effects of the alcohol. "I can just show you. "

Theresa let out a shrill scream in readiness.

"Hold on, let me grab the remote. "I reached on the table for the remote, guided the television to the Pay-Per-View menu and went to the "Adult" section. I picked the title of the movie that I had masturbated to a few days before and pressed Play.

The same beautiful women who brought me to pleasure earlier appeared on the screen and started kissing while slowly caressing each other.

"Oh my God!I cannot believe what I'm seeing," she yelled.

I immediately began to feel self-conscious and went to turn the TV off.

"What are you doing?"She looked at me like I was crazy.

"I'm about to turn it off, I can't believe I just did that. "

"Girl, no you are not!C'mon, let's watch!"

I sat back down, but felt immediately defensive. Theresa noticed the change in my energy, and she put her hand on my thigh as Redbone and Blondie's moans pierced through the silence.

"Christy, have I ever judged you before?"

"No," I said without looking her in the eye.

"Well, why would I judge you now?Now, I was just joking,

and I'm sorry if I offended you. I was just excited about this new facet of you that I just found out about. That's all. I masturbate too, everyone does. It's no big deal, and I promise, I do not look at you differently. "

I hugged her and kissed her on the cheek. "Thanks, it's just that I have never told anyone about it. "

"But why?"

I gestured toward the television. "Just look at it. "

At that time, Petite was sitting on Redbone's face while Blondie was squeezing and twisting Petite's nipples. In ecstasy, Petite moaned and said, "Eat my pussy. "

Theresa shrugged. "Yeah, so?"

"Reesey, turn around and look at it. "

She finally did, and then I could tell that it dawned on her the reason why I felt like I should keep it a secret.

"Because it's lesbian porn?"

"Yeah. "I nodded.

"I don't know why you're ashamed. Girl, this shit is hot!Look at that one!"

There was a close-up of Blondie with her legs up to her ears. While Redbone's tongue slowly and deliberately dragged across her vagina in a back-and-forth motion.

Then, as if I could read Theresa's mind, I saw a thought popped into her head.

She said, "Do you think that you're a lesbian?Is that why you're hesitant to tell people?"

"Nah... well, I don't know. Here's my logic behind it:I think I like lesbian porn because the guy-girl ones are... so misogynist. You know?You can tell that it's made to entertain men and what they find appealing. But look at that. "I gestured to a new scene with Redbone and Petite on a white suede couch. Petite was eating Redbone's pussy while fingering her at the same time. Petite had her eyes closed and a smile on her face. It was clear that she was enjoying eating Redbone's pussy.

"These girls don't look like they're doing it for men, even if they are. It's so passionate, and it's really how a girl wants to be eaten. Girl, Reginald once took my clit in his mouth and just started shaking his head like a dog. Like it was supposed to do something. "

"Wait?He did what?"She turned away from the TV and looked at me, clamping her knees together as if she could feel my pain.

"Yeah. But these women look like they actually know what they're doing, and that's what turns me on. I love getting my pussy ate, and they do it so well. "

"Oh my God, they do. Look at that one. "

There was a close-up of Blondie interchanging between licking and sucking on Petite's clit. When Blondie pulled away slightly, you could see that Petite's clit was enlarged from the attention and the pleasure she was receiving.

I immediately got moist and wished that I could grab my vibrator.

Theresa said, "But that still doesn't answer my previous question. Do you think that you might be a lesbian?"

I thought for a second. "Well, if someone thinks about stealing but never does it, does that make them a thief?"

Theresa laughed when she realized what I was alluding to. "No, it does not. "

"So no, I don't think I am. But—" I reached over and took another large gulp from my Jack and soda. "—I got to be honest; before I completely give up dating, relationships and sex I think I would like to have sex with a woman, at least once. "

"Have you ever fooled around with a girl before?"She looked at me, her eyes wide with wonder and excitement.

"No, but I have had opportunities, though. "

Theresa began laughing. "Oh my God, what happened?"

"Well, there was one time in high school this girl who I was friends with used to say… stuff. "

"What kind of stuff?"Theresa said, nudging me with her elbow.

"Things like, 'You're so beautiful, I would love to see how you look when you have sex. '"

"What?"

"Yeah!And she would sometimes come up behind me, put her hand on my back and say 'If I was touching the front of you, I would be touching your breasts'. "

"Oh my God!"

"Yeah, and once this butch girl, started hitting on me at the bus stop when I was coming home from the mall in college. Oh!Do you remember Karen?She lived in Fulton?You know the grad dorms?"

"Yeah. "

"Well, I had a class with her and she invited me to come and study, and more. "

"Oh my God!And what did you used to say when this happened?"

"Umm… 'No thank you. But thanks anyway'. "

Theresa and I both exploded with laughter. Theresa bent over and grabbed her drink, took a large sip, and continued her questioning: "Well, if you had all of those opportunities, why not take them?"

I looked at the TV, and Blondie was riding Redbone's face. As she did, she rubbed her thighs in ecstasy, and the clip went to a close-up of Redbone's tongue, as it flicked between the lips of Blondie's pussy.

"Those times just didn't seem right. With the girl from high school… I don't know, I felt like she just liked saying stuff to sort of shock people. I didn't know if she was serious. The girl at the mall, no. If I'm gonna be with a girl, I want her to look like a girl. As for the girl at school, I don't know, you know. I feel like you have to really trust who you do something like that with. You know how fast rumors start, especially on our campus. And who's to say that out of spite she wouldn't tell anyone?"

"It seems like your standards are a little too high," she said, then burst into hysterical laughter as she watched Blondie and Redbone grind their vaginas to ecstasy. "Look at them go!"

"Really, Reesey, do you think that you could do something like that with just anyone?"

She sat back and thought for a second. "Honestly, no. I mean, I've kissed a girl or two as a dare, but yeah, having sex with one makes it a little trickier. "

I took the remote and switched to another girl-on-girl movie that opened with two women who started out on a couch kissing and rubbing each other's breasts. After each woman helped ease the other out of their shirts, they both took turns sucking on each other's nipples.

"The thing is, you want someone who you can trust, and some-one who won't make you feel weird afterward. Someone who you're close to, but not someone who is close enough that you're like sisters. That's where the problem lies. "

Theresa got a glazed look in her eyes as she thought about it, as if she was fully engaged in the conversation, but also trying to solve a math problem at the same time. I blamed it all on the alcohol and kept on talking.

"If there weren't so many diseases out there, I would try to go to a lesbian club. But then again people are crazy nowadays. You pick someone up at the club and you're lucky if they don't kill you, or at least rob you. Plus, what do you say if you run into someone you know?"

Theresa laughed and pushed me, almost losing her balance. Yes, she was sort of tipsy. The two women in the movie were now fully naked, and the one with the straight long hair had her face buried into the pussy of the one with the long curled hair. The one with the straight hair kept on pushing the other's leg open to show off her divine licking techniques. As the other began to writhe in pleasure, the one giving it to her wouldn't stop, and continued as her mouth followed the pussy as it began to rhythmically and slowly bounce up and down.

"Well, it was just a thought, but I guess I won't be doing it. I don't mind masturbating to my porn. Now come on, you wanna keep on watching this, or would you like to switch to a real movie?"

Theresa took one glimpse at the TV screen, and the one with the long curly hair was eating the other's pussy while also fingering it. "Christy, it's your weekend, so whatever you want to do, I'll do it. "

I picked up the remote and turned the Pay-Per-View movie off. "You know, there was a movie that Reginald wouldn't let me go to the movies to see. I actually got it on bootleg and I've been so eager to watch it. "

"Let's do it!"Theresa cheered, but all the while that look of concentration and thought came on her.

* * *

After the movie was over I turned to Theresa. "Okay, so you wanna do another movie?You can pick this time. "

Theresa stood up and grabbed my hand. "Actually, you wanna

watch the next movie in the bedroom?So we can really relax?"

"That sounds great. I love my couch, but nothing beats a nice mattress. "We walked down the hallway to my room. "Did you like the movie?"

"Yeah, it was cool," she answered, but I could tell that something was on her mind.

"What's wrong, Reesey?Is my darling sick from all the champagne?"I said, as I grabbed her arm and walked hand in hand with her while resting my head on her shoulder.

"Nah, I stopped drinking when the movie came on. I'm kind of sobering up now. "

"That's great, me too!"We walked in and I immediately, out of habit, I took my shorts off in preparation of getting into bed. I sat down on my side of the bed and placed a pillow behind me so I could be comfortable sitting against the headboard.

"Christy, I've been thinking about something," Theresa said thoughtfully as she made her way to my side of the bed.

I looked at her and tried to read her mind. This time, I was blocked out; I couldn't tell what she was thinking.

"Well, have you been having fun this weekend?"She said, walking closer to me.

"Of course. You're amazing!This is one of the best weekends I've had in a long time!"

"That's great!"She smiled at me, but she kept on walking closer, and then sat on the bed in front of me. "Well, this weekend was supposed to be for your freedom and being an opportunity for you to be able to do all the things you wanted to do. Well, I would feel like a horrible friend if I didn't completely abide by that promise. "

I looked at her confused. I went dancing, just ate my weight in pizza, had champagne, and a delicious cake. What else could I want? "What do you mean?"

"Well, do you trust me, Christy?"

"Of course I do, you know that. "

Theresa slowly leaned forward and kissed me. Shocked, I didn't move back or kiss back. I just let the kiss happen. She pulled away from me and smiled. "Do you feel weird?"

I thought about it. I honestly didn't, but my heart was racing. Was this really about to happen?"No, I don't feel weird. "

"Do you think I'm going to rob you?"She teased.

"No, not like I have anything of value here anyway. "I laughed.

She leaned back and took her shirt off and then her bra, exposing her perky breasts and erect nipples. Even though I'd seen her naked this weekend, this was different. This was with the intention of having sex, and they did look delicious. I wanted to touch them, rub them, bring her nipples to my mouth to suck on them, but I felt paralyzed.

She looked at me and said:"May I?" She gestured to my shirt and bra as well.

I nodded, not knowing what to say. She slowly grabbed the bottom of my shirt and worked it over my body toward my head. I closed my eyes and became hyper aware of everything around me. The way her perfume smelled; how her fingers grazed my body as they carried the shirt up; how soft her hands were. After the shirt was completely off, she leaned forward and rested her head on my shoulder as she gently unbuckled my bra. I felt as the weight of my titties came down slightly from being supported by the bra, and I felt the cool air hit my bare chest as she removed my bra. My eyes were still closed. I was afraid of what might happen if I looked at her. Would I turn into stone? Would I feel humiliated and chicken out? What if she was disgusted by my body? What was I doing? Am I really about to do this?

"Christy, please open your eyes," she said.

I opened my eyes, and the first thing I saw was the vulnerability in hers. Fear that maybe I would look at her differently after she just offered herself to me. Fear that maybe I was just joking, and how could our friendship survive this if she took it too far?

"Reesey, you have a great rack," I joked and we both burst out laughing.

"Thank you, Christy," she said and began caressing my titties. "You do too. "Then her mouth found my right nipple. As she sucked on my right nipple, her hand found my left and began to squeeze and twist it.

I felt my panties getting moist. Her mouth felt amazing as she sucked my nipple and then went to the other. She squeezed my breasts together and then flicked the nipples with her tongue. My hand began caressing her bare back while she attended to my nipples, and my other hand began to fondle her breasts. She let out a sigh of pleasure.

She slowly lifted up, and all I could think about was fitting her perfect-looking breasts in my mouth. I caressed her titties and lowered my head to the right nipple. As I took it into my mouth, she sucked in a quick breath. I began sucking the nipple and occasionally flicking it with my tongue. Then I moved to the other one while caressing and squeezing the one my mouth had just been with.

"Oh my God," she moaned.

I rose up and our eyes met.

Both saying the same thing, but to confirm, Theresa said, "Are you okay?"

I answered by kissing her. I knew that if I stuck to my vow to never have sex, date, or be in a relationship, then I wouldn't be able to kiss anyone else, so I decided to make the kiss as passionate as I could. Our tongues danced with each other, and we occasionally took turns sucking on the other's tongue.

She gently pushed me back on the mattress, and then she slowly moved her mouth from mine and onto my neck. Her kisses were soft, gentle, but hungry to devour my chocolate skin. She moved down my neck back to my nipples, and then she slowly went down my stomach.

My heart began to race as I realized where she was heading. She gripped the top of my purple laced panties and began to pull them down. To help her, I raised my pelvis and she slid them all the way off my body and tossed them on the floor. She opened my thighs, exposing my pussy, and began to kiss the inside of my thigh where my knees were and worked her way toward my pussy. Right when she was about to get there, she started kissing the inside of my other thigh, this time going toward my knee, and my body began to shake with desire. Gripping my breasts and squeezing my nipples with my fingertips, I awaited the moment I daydreamed about while laying on my bed masturbating.

Before I realized it, the warmth of her mouth met my clit, and I immediately felt like I was about to melt. As if she had done this many times, she slowly licked my clit. Warm sensations danced up my body as her tongue danced on and around my hot button of desire. I felt her fingers as they opened my lips and gave her better access to my clit, and she took advantage of it.

I began grinding my pussy in her face while also squeezing my breasts and nipples. I looked down at her, and our eyes made contact as she sucked on my clit. As she sucked, I began to feel my temperature rise and then a tingling sensation in my feet.

Before I could comprehend what was about to happen, she suddenly plunged her tongue into my warm slit, and I could feel her tongue dancing with my insides. At that moment, I grabbed her head and pulled it into me. No man had ever made the space between my thighs feel as amazing as Theresa was. As I let her head go, her hands caressed up my body and they found my breasts.

She pulled her tongue out of my pussy and went back to licking and sucking my clit. Slow and gentle at first, but she started picking up the speed and sucking harder as she went along. The tingling feeling appeared in my feet again, and then turned into warmth. The warmth traveled up my body as her tongue moved faster and faster on my clit. She quickly squeezed my nipples as her mouth danced with my pussy while my body rose. Before I knew it, I screamed as I had the most powerful orgasmic explosions I had ever encountered. She pulled back and looked at me in amazement. My body was shaking with pleasure, and I became hyper sensitive to the touch. I looked at her and pulled her on top of me and began kissing her. I could still taste my pussy on her tongue, and it actually got me excited to return the favor to her.

I cupped my hands underneath her ass and pulled her forward until her breasts were at my mouth. As her nipples dangled above my lips, I lifted my head to meet them. Opening my mouth, I let my tongue slip out and caress the areola while her titties still swung in my face. Then, I took the whole nipple in my mouth. Theresa moaned and grabbed the back of my head and brought it to her breasts.

She moaned as she rubbed her hands through my loose curls. I lay my head on the pillow as she lowered her titties toward my mouth. I hungrily accepted them, as if they were the nourishment I always craved, and sucked them while palming them at the same time. I then pulled her farther up until she was in a crouching position over my face. I helped her to lower her freshly waxed pussy to my mouth and licked her clit. Her pussy lips seemed to open, exposing her clit to me, and I slowly licked and sucked it while my hands continued to play with and squeeze her breasts.

"Oh my God… Christy… you are so good," she said with a moan as she started to rock back and forth.

Determined to make her cum as hard as I had, my mouth followed, and I refused to break contact with her clit.

My tongue danced and played with her clit, while occasionally sucking it. As my tongue moved back and forth, I searched for her opening. Once I found it, I plunged my tongue inside. She immediately stopped rocking and put her hands over my hands, which were fondling her smooth breasts.

"Oh my God!"She yelled and started feverishly rocking.

I darted my tongue in and out, and then decided to go back to her hot button of ecstasy. I went back to licking it and gently sucking it while caressing and squeezing her breasts. I sped up my tongue action and gradually sucked harder. As I did, I squeezed her nipples harder, and she rocked harder and moaned louder.

I felt the weight of her body shift as she threw her head back. I could feel her clit become engorged in my mouth so I knew that she was close to climaxing. My tongue started working faster, feeling the blood rushing to the clit that was dancing in my mouth with desire. I could hear the slow guttural growl of desire coming out of her mouth and gradually getting louder and louder as she came. I felt a small rush of fluid drain from her pussy and onto my chin as she climaxed.

The room became silent and still. I removed my hands from her breasts. Even though I was no longer touching them, I could still feel my hands around them, and the sensation of how taut her nipples felt between my fingers. She rose from my face slightly and slid off to the left side of the bed. She slowly climbed under the covers and lay down, staring at the ceiling, speechless. We both fell asleep, letting the last sounds we heard from our conscious minds, being her scream of desire as she climaxed.

* * *

The next morning we woke up and showered separately. Even though we didn't mention what happened, it was obvious that the topic was on both of our minds and at the tips of our tongues.

Theresa had to be back at the train station by twelve noon so we decided to just go out to a pancake café around ten that morning. We sat down at the table and talked pleasantly, but I felt awkward when our hands mistakenly brushed against each other while reaching for the same condiments. Even through the midst of uneasiness, Theresa continued to smile at me with eyes that communicated that I shouldn't feel weird about what happened and that she'd always be my friend. I just hoped that my eyes and smile told her the same thing.

Once our breakfast was done and we were back in the car heading toward the train station, she turned to me, "I understand if you don't want to talk about last night, but I just wanted to let you know that you're still one of my friends... well, best friends after last night. "We both burst into laughter after that comment. "But I just wanted to let you know that it doesn't have to be weird between us. If you want, we can just pretend like nothing happened, or we can talk about it. It's all up to you. "

I listened silently. Not knowing what to say. I nodded in agreement that she's still my friend, but I didn't know if she was just telling me things to get me comfortable or not. We continued to ride in comfortable silence to the train station. By that time, we just accepted what happened the night before and there was no need to feel ashamed about it, because it happened and we couldn't take it back.

"Do you want me to walk you in?"I said, getting ready to turn into the parking lot.

Theresa turned and smiled. "No thanks, you know that you can't even get that far with security checks nowadays. But thank you, though. "

She turned toward the door and put her hand on the handle. I placed my hand on her thigh to stop her and to get her attention. She turned toward me and smiled, waiting to hear what I was going to say.

"Reesey, I just wanted to let you know that you are one of the best friends I have ever had. Thank you so much for an amazing weekend. Everything was perfect, and I hope you can come down again soon. "

Theresa giggled and said, "How does next month sound?"

I smiled. "That sounds like a plan. Thanks again for everything. "

We gave each other a knowing smile, and she opened up the door.

"I'll see you in a month, Hun!"She called out as she grabbed her bag. "I'll be calling you soon. "

"Please call me when you get home, so I know you didn't crash or something. "

"I promise I will. "She waved and shut the door.

As she bounced to the automatic doors, she turned one last time and gave me a wave. I watched her go to the counter to hand the people her ticket, and then I pulled off and drove toward the exit.

As I drove away a smile spread across my face. Though I didn't know what road my life was going to lead to, especially with the steps that Theresa and I took last night, I knew that I had a spectacular friend that was going to be there for me. Whether or not we ever decided to follow-up on that night's events, it'll always be our little secret.

You Belong To Me

By Keisha Ervin

Dedication

This story is dedicated to all of the hopeless romantics. Who know the love of your life might be right underneath your nose.

PROLOGUE: 2008

After a long, brutal day of receiving verbal bitch slaps from her boss, line assistant, Nicolette Williams, sat irritably awaiting her blind date Kenzo. They were scheduled to meet at 7:00 PM at Miso, a sushi restaurant in St. Louis, for dinner, but it was 7:20 and Kenzo hadn't arrived or called to say he would be running late. If it hadn't been for her best friend, Madison's, big approval rating of him, Nik would have been stepped. Besides that, it had been months since Nik had been on a date so she was in desperate need for some male companionship.

There was only so much her rabbit vibrator could do. Although it satisfied the itch that needed to be scratched, a vibrator couldn't whisper naughty words in her ear, kiss her lips, or kneed her breasts. A woman needed physical contact and if Kenzo played his cards right, he might be the man to get inside of Nik's warm honey pot. Beyond annoyed by his tardiness, Nik gazed down at her watch, 7:30 PM.

This fool got five more minutes and I'm out. Then, as she took a small sip of her water, the door to the restaurant swung open and a tall drink of chocolate milk came walking through the door. Nik couldn't believe her eyes. Madison said he was fine but goddamn, this man was fine beyond words. He was six feet tall and looked to be almost two hundred pounds. Spinning waves ran throughout his jet black hair. Smoldering almond-shaped eyes, a regal nose, and a goatee made up his facial features.

Physically, he was one of God's greatest creations. But his attire, to Nik, was less than desirable. Kenzo looked like a twenty-eight-year-old stickup kid. Since it was winter, he rocked a blue Yankee's cap, a blue oversized hoodie with a tee shirt on underneath, baggy denim jeans, and a pair of wheat Timberland boots. Nik didn't know whether to duck for cover or introduce herself. Deciding to go with the latter, she stood up and smoothed down her skirt. Despite his appearance, Nik found herself unable to take her eyes off the huge bulge in the center of his jeans. That let her know he was working with a monster. *Maybe I won't have to cuss Madison out after all.*

"What up, chocolate?" Kenzo took her into his arms and hugged her tight.

Nik wasn't the type of chick that he normally went for because of her minimal makeup and conservative attire, but beyond the blah exterior, he couldn't get pass how stunningly beautiful she was. Nik was a 5'9" statuesque Barbie doll with skin the color of Godiva chocolate. Her long, coal black hair was pulled back into a single ponytail that reached the middle of her back. She possessed doe-shaped eyes and sensuous lips that he yearned to kiss.

"It's Nik. My name is Nik. " She stepped back. "And you must be Kenzo. " She gave him a half-hearted smile.

"Yep, that's my government, but you can call me Zo. " He took a seat.

"Kenzo's fine," Nik replied, taken aback that he didn't pull out her chair. "You do realize that you're a half an hour late. " She sat down and placed her napkin across her lap.

"My bad. I got caught up in the studio. "

"Oh, so you're one of those?" Nik rolled her eyes.

"One of what?" Kenzo said perplexed.

"A rapper?"

"No, I'm an actor. I had to do some voice-over work. I just got a small role in this movie called Precious. I used to get into rap but the acting bug bit me," Kenzo said.

"Oh... isn't that special. " Nik looked over the menu unimpressed.

Noticing the sour expression on her face, Kenzo said, "What? You got something against rappers?"

"No, as a matter of fact, I'm a huge fan of rap. Every now and then I'll bust out a lil' Will Smith or LL. "

"You do realize its 2008, don't you?" Kenzo looked at her in disbelief. "You don't listen to Wayne or Kanye?"

"Absolutely not. " Nik shook her head. "Lil' Wayne is a cough syrup sippin,' Bob Marley wannabe; and Kanye is a narcissistic, arrogant, asshole. "

"Wow. " Kenzo chuckled, outdone. "On that note, have you ordered yet?"

"No. I was trying to be polite and wait on you," Nik shot back sarcastically.

"That's what's up," Kenzo said oblivious to her dig. "Ay yo, Garcon. "He snapped his fingers, signaling the waiter.

"You have got to be kidding me. " Nik covered the side of her face with her hand, embarrassed.

"Sir?" the waiter said.

"Let me get a Hennessey and coke," Kenzo instructed. "What you want, Miss Lady?"

"Nik, my name is Nik," she said. "I'll have a Sprite, please. " She looked at the waiter.

"Coming right up. " The waiter nodded.

"You don't drink?" Kenzo was surprised.

"No. "

"I bet that's not your real hair either. "He smirked.

"Actually it is. " Nik screwed up her face.

"Word? What you take like pregnancy pills or something to get it that long?" Kenzo leaned forward and eyed her quizzically.

"No. " Nik's upper lip curled.

"Oh. " Kenzo shrugged his shoulders and sat back in his chair.

"This is gonna be a long night," Nik mumbled.

"What you say?"

"Nothing. "Nik waved him off.

"So why you think yo' homegirl wanted to set us up?" Zo sat back in his seat.

"I have no idea. I've been wondering why this entire time. "

"Real talk, me too. I mean, yo' homegirl hella cool. She's a good look for Keith. "

"Keith is a great guy. How are you two friends? Because you

two are just … so different," Nik said, dying to know.

"He's my brother. And how are we so different?"

"Keith's just so refined—"

"Keep-A-Bitch Keith?" Kenzo chuckled. "Please, Keith is just as hood as I am. "

"I find that hard to believe," Nik scoffed.

"Then you don't know Keith then. And what you trying' to say? 'Cause he work on Wall Street and wear a suit and a tie every day that he better than me?" Kenzo was offended.

"You said it. I didn't. " Nik arched her eyebrow.

"See, this why I don't do shit like this. 'Cause bourgeoisie chicks like you get under my skin," he barked.

"I'm far from bourgeoisie, sweetheart. " Nik folded her arms across her chest.

"Man, please. The stick you got up yo' ass is so long its choking' you!"

Nik's jaw instantly dropped. "You know what?" She slapped down her napkin on the table. People around them stared but she didn't care. She'd had enough. It was time to put Kenzo in his place once and for all. "I have better things to do with my time then to sit here and be attacked! First, you were late. You have no manners and you're dressed like a reject from The Wire. So frankly, my dear, you can kiss my ass!" Nik scooted back her chair.

"What ass? I've seen fatter asses on Asian women. " Kenzo laughed.

Appalled, Nik gasped for air. "Fuck you!" she hissed, grabbing her purse.

"I'm good shorty. You're not my type. " Kenzo waved her off.

"That's the first thing you've said all night that we can agree on. " Nik stood up. "Goodnight douche bag!"

"That's why you look like Condoleezza Rice, trick," Kenzo yelled over his shoulder as she stormed out.

ONE

Three Years Later

"Uh-uh-uh," Nik moaned while riding up and down on her boy-friend Greg's dick.

For almost thirty minutes she'd tried her damnest to cum but the closer she came to bliss the quicker it seemed to disappear. Maybe it was because she was about to come face to face with her arch nemesis after three years. Since their date from hell, she'd moved to New York and became an executive producer for the Ego network and created such hits for the network like The Millionaire Wives' Club, Skeezer Scavenger Hunt, and Who Wants to Be a Porn Star?

Nik wished she could've produced more profound pieces, but reality shows made money and the network wanted hits. So despite her vast knowledge of politics, foreign policies, and documentary work, she had to deliver. Greg, on the other hand, despised her work and begged her on numerous occasions to quit and allow him to take care of her. But Nik was no kept woman. Since birth she'd been raised to be self-sufficient.

Sure Greg had more money than Brad Pitt and Beyoncé combined, but none of that mattered to Nik. She loved him for his charming ways, debonair style, and take-control attitude. Unlike Nik, he'd grown up wealthy. Greg was like the black John F.

Kennedy Jr. His father was a judge for the Supreme Court and his mother was hotelier and socialite Judith Steiner.

Greg, himself, was the other owner and CEO of his very own energy drink. He was everything a woman could dream for. He was rich, powerful, and handsome, but no matter how much Nik tried to ignore it, there was just something messing between them.

"Lay down." Greg grabbed her waist and laid her on her back.

In the missionary position, Nik wrapped her arms around Greg's neck. With her eyes closed, she tried to match his rhythm in order to cum, but once again she became distracted.

"What time is it?" she said.

Greg looked over at the clock. "Six o'clock, why?" He panted.

"We need to hurry up. I have a million things to do."

"You're joking, right?" Greg looked at her face.

"No, so nut now or forever hold your peace." Nik patted his back.

"Can you please find another word to use besides nut? It's so crass." Greg continued to stroke.

"Sorry, can you please ejaculate so we can go?" Nik rolled her eyes.

While Greg rolled his hips in a circular motion and worked her middle, all Nik could think about was finishing packing, making sure she had her passport, getting to the airport on time, and arriving at Neckar Island for her best friend Madison and Keith's wedding. It was too bad she'd have to share the wonderful occasion with Kenzo.

"Ooh," Greg groaned, pumping faster, causing Nik's head to hit the headboard.

"I'm cumming," he said.

Not in the least bit turned on, Nik gazed at the wall in anticipation of him finishing and her getting up.

"Ah," Greg groaned as his body shuttered and he came. "Whew. " He pulled out of her and slumped over onto his side. "I don't know about you, but I feel great. "He smiled.

"Good for you. " Nik stood up and put on her robe. "Now get up. We don't have any more time to waste. We have to pack our suitcases, shower, dress, and make it to the airport in less than an hour and a half. " Nik went into her closet and pulled out her Louis Vuitton luggage.

"I didn't know us making love was wasting time, but all right. " Greg got up, slightly pissed.

"I wasn't saying it like that, honey. " Nik tried to clean it up.

"It's okay. " Greg went into the bathroom to throw away the condom they'd used.

"No, it's not. " Nik took his hand once he returned to the room. "I apologize. I'm just so overwhelmed. "

"I know you are. That's why you have to calm down. This is supposed to be a relaxing five day vacay. "

"For you but not for me. I still have the bachelor/bachelorette party to plan since Kenzo hasn't lifted a finger to help, except for writing a check. As a matter of fact, let me call him now and see if he's hired the belly dancers like he promised. "

"Don't you think it's a bit early?" Greg said.

"I don't care. He should be up anyway. " Nik dialed his number. "I'll probably speak to his assistant anyway since he won't bother to speak to me himself. "

"Hello? This is Kenzo Porter's assistant Janet, how may I help you?"

"Good morning, Janet, this is Nik. Is Kenzo available?"

"Actually. " Janet paused. "He's not. Is there anything that I can help you with?"

"Yes. I wanted to know if he's hired the belly dancers for the bachelor/bachelorette party yet? The party is just days away. "

"Um, I don't think so, but I will make sure that it is taken care of. "

"Please do, Janet. I would really appreciate it. "

"No problem, and let me know if there is anything else I can help you with. "

"I probably will, knowing your boss," Nik said, hanging up. "Ugh! I can't stand him!" She raised her hands to the sky.

"What?" Greg said, while picking out underwear.

"He hasn't done anything I've asked him to do. I swear to God when I see him I might punch him in the face. " Nik fought the air.

"You will do no such thing. " Greg held her by her arms. "Kenzo is a very busy man. He's the highest paid actor in the world right now. I'm sure he doesn't have time to plan some stupid party. "

"Um, excuse me, but my best friend's bachelorette party is not stupid. " Nik removed his hands from her arms. "And Kenzo isn't any busier than I am. I know it's not a big deal to you, but I do run one of televisions' biggest networks. "

"Your words not mine. " Greg went into the bathroom and turned on the shower.

"Whatever. Just hurry up so we can go!"

* * *

"Kenzo! Kenzo!" Janet nudged his back. "Kenzo wake up! You're going to miss your flight!"

"Huh?" He scrunched up his face and tried opening his eyes.

"You have to get up. The car is outside waiting for you. "

"I'm up. I'm up. " Kenzo turned onto his side and spotted a naked Hispanic woman asleep.

"Whoa," he said, sitting up only to find a caramel cutie at the foot of his bed.

"Baby, where are you going?" The white woman on his left whined.

Kenzo had no recollection of bedding the three beauties the night before. The whole night was an entire blur. But from the looks of his bedroom, he had a hell of a time. There were red plastic cups, beer bottles, lube, a set of handcuffs, and Magnum Trojan condoms scattered everywhere.

"Yeah, the rest of the house looks even worse," Janet said, reading his mind.

"Cool. " Kenzo grinned, pleased with himself.

"Come on, you're running super late. " Janet urged out of bed.

"Okay. " Kenzo got out of bed.

"No, baby, come back. " The Hispanic woman pouted. "Don't you wanna play with these?" She pressed her titties together.

"I wish I could but I gotta go right now. " Kenzo eyed her big luscious breasts.

"Aw, no fair. " The Hispanic woman hit the pillow with a fist.

"Enough of this foolishness, you have to get in the shower now or you won't make it to your brother's wedding. " Janet pushed Kenzo toward the master bath.

"Oh, and by the way, Nik called again. You forgot to tell me to hire belly dancers for the party. "

"Damn, I did," Kenzo said, taking off his boxer briefs.

"Do you have any shame?" Janet covered her eyes and turned around.

"Not when I look this good. " Kenzo admired his muscular frame in the mirror.

"I've seen better," Janet teased.

"Who you foolin'?" Kenzo smirked.

Janet simply smiled because she knew he was right. "Anyway, she seemed pretty upset. "

"That sounds about right. " Kenzo turned on the hot water.

"You have exactly ten minutes to shower and dress," Janet said, closing the door behind her.

Kenzo opened the shower door and got in. The hot, steamy water instantly woke him up and made him wish Nik was enjoying the sensation with him. It had been three years since they'd come face to face. But images of her angelic face often resurfaced in his mind. Sure, on the night of their date he'd been a dick and she'd been an uppity bitch. But beyond her holier-than-thou attitude, he saw a woman full of potential.

Physically she was a ten. It was her mouth he couldn't get with. He wondered if after all this time she'd changed and loosened up a bit. But by the sound of Janet's messages she hadn't. Kenzo just prayed they'd be able to get along long enough to support her best friend and his brother during the biggest moment of their lives without killing each other.

* * *

"Wow, this is beautiful," Nik gleamed, stepping down off of the boat.

Neckar Island, Billionaire Richard Branson's villa, where Madison and Keith's nuptials would take place, was breathtaking. It was completely secluded and every couples' dream wedding location. It was a seventy-four acre, private, paradise on the British Virgin Islands. The main house where all of the guests were staying held ten bedrooms, an indoor and outdoor dining area, Balinese-styled interiors for lounging, and a reading and games area with a full-size snooker table.

A staff of thirty-one was there to pamper the guests at all times. Nik couldn't wait to let her hair down and enjoy all of the amenities the villa had to offer. Holding Greg's hand, she led him across the pristine white sand to greet Madison and Keith.

"Friend!" Madison extended her arms wide and ran toward Nik.

"Bestie!" Nik held out her arms as well.

"I missed you. " Madison hugged her tight.

"I missed you too. " Nik held her at arm's length and gazed at her lovingly.

"Do you love it or do you love it?" Madison gushed.

"This is sick, Maddie. I mean, beyond fabulous. " Nik was in awe. "And look at you. You look great. "

Maddie was a pint-sized caramel cutie. Her entire being exuded sex appeal and her attire often reflected it. The purple halter beach dress she rocked highlighted her 34 D breast implants and showcased enough leg to make any red blooded man look twice.

"I try. " Madison posed like a supermodel. "You, on the other hand, friend, look a hotmess. com. What happened to your hair?"

"I don't know. " Nik tried to control her mane unsuccessfully. "It just poofed up like an afro. This heat is ridiculous, girl. I'm sweating like Whitney Houston on stage. " She fanned her armpits.

"Um-mm. " Greg cleared his throat.

"Oh, babe, I'm sorry. " Nik took him by the hand and pulled him toward her. "Madison, this is my boyfriend, Greg that I've gone on and on about; and, Greg, this is my best friend, Madison. "

"Nice to meet you. I've heard so much about you. " He greeted her with a warm hug.

"So have I, and I would like for you to meet my soon-to-be-husband Keith. " Madison smiled up at her fiancé.

"Nice to meet you. " Keith shook his hand.

"We have so much to go over. " Madison's sweet demeanor vanished and a more serious side of her appeared. "There is so much more that needs to be done and my wedding planner, honey, is working' my nerves. "

"I got you. Everything's gonna be fine. You're gonna have the most beautiful wedding ever, I promise," Nik swore.

"Thanks, girl. I needed that. "

"Uh-oh, here comes trouble. " Keith boasted, looking toward the ocean.

Nik followed his gaze and found Kenzo along with a few other guests getting off of another boat.

This shit isn't fair, Nik thought. While she looked like a refugee, Kenzo looked as if he'd stepped right out of an ad campaign. The man looked better than he did three years before. Money and fame really agreed with him. Instead of rocking' waves in his hair, he now sported a low cut and his goatee had been replaced with a full, luscious beard that framed his kissable lips well.

Damn, I wanna kiss him. Nik gazed at him absentmindedly. No you don't! Remember, he's an asshole?Okay, get it together. He is not all that. Smoothing her hair back for the one hundredth time,

157

Nik plastered on a fake smile as Kenzo neared.

"What up, nigga?" Kenzo greeted Keith with a hug.

"You, Mr. Box Office. " Keith hugged him back. "Me and Madison just went to see Unbreakable. You did yo' thang, man. "

"Yeah, they say I might get nominated for a Golden Globe. "

"Oh, most definitely. "

"Excuse me, Mr. Porter, but can I please have your autograph?" one of Madison's bridesmaids nervously said.

Nik wanted to hate on the chick but she was gorgeous. The woman was everything Nik wasn't. She was short and built like a brick house.

"Damn. " Greg admired her frame. He was eyeing her so hard he was practically drooling.

"Excuse you. " Nik nudged him.

"What?" He shrugged, trying to play it off.

"Who do you want me to make this out to, sweetheart?" Kenzo stared deep into the woman's eyes.

"Laila. " The woman swooned.

"You got a piece of paper, Miss Laila?"

"No. You can sign right here. " Laila pulled the neck of her top to the side, revealing the upper part of her right breast.

"I think I'm gonna throw up. " Nik rolled her eyes unaware that Kenzo heard her.

"Ay, Keith? You smell that?" Kenzo sniffed the air, handing

Laila back her pen.

"Smell what?" Keith looked around curiously.

"I smell a hater in the air. " Kenzo shot daggers at Nik with his eyes. "What's up, junk in the trunk?"

"For the millionth time, my name is Nik," she snapped.

"Oh my bad, Nicole. "

"It's Nicolette, fool!"

"Whatever, it's all the same," Kenzo teased.

"Are you two gonna fight the whole time?" Madison said, hugging Kenzo.

"That's her. " He pointed like a child.

"What are you, nine?" Nik curled her upper lip.

"No, but my dick is. " Kenzo cracked up laughing.

"All right, that's it. " Nik threw up her hands defeated. "I'm going to my room! Greg!" she yelled over her shoulder as she stormed off.

"But I haven't even got to speak to Kenzo yet. You know I'm a huge fan. "

"Are you insane?" Nik whispered, walking into his personal space. "The man just insulted me. "

"Well, you did kinda start it. " Greg shrugged.

"You know what? Do you!" Nik spat, grabbing her own luggage.

"It was nice meeting you all. " Greg picked up his bags and ran after Nik.

"You better leave my friend alone. " Madison laughed.

"She'll be a'ight. " Kenzo waved his hand dismissively.

TWO

Fatal Attraction

Alone in their room Nik spun around on her heels, scaring Greg half to death, and said, "Why didn't you stand up for me?"

"What was I supposed to say, Nik? The man was just joking. " He sat their bags down on the floor.

"You don't understand. That man is the bane of my existence. I detest him. The sight of his face makes my skin crawl. "Her body shook profusely.

"Honestly, I think you're carrying on a bit. " Greg examined the room.

"Oh, really?" Nik arched her eyebrow. "You think I'm carrying on? It's cool. "She sucked her teeth. "That's what's up. "

"Okay, you can stop with all of that ghetto mess. You know I don't like it. If you're going to talk to me, speak correct English, please. "

"Let me go then, since I'm carrying on too much and can't speak correct English!" Nik left the room, slamming the door behind her.

Hot and aggravated she knocked on Madison's bedroom door.

"Come in!"

"Ugh, I hate him. " Nik stormed inside.

"Hate who?" Madison said, unpacking her bag.

"Kenzo. He's such a dick. " Nik plopped down on the bed.

"Not tryin' to be a bitch, but you did start it. " Madison pointed out.

"I know I did, but so what. He's a total douche bag whore. I swear I've never met someone who was so conceited. "

"For you not to like him so much, he's surely the main topic of your conversation. " Madison laughed.

"It's not funny, Madison," Nik whined. "He hasn't even helped with the bachelor/bachelorette party. I've had to do everything on my own. He won't even answer my calls when I call him. I have to speak to his assistant. Like he's such a big superstar that he can't even speak to me. "

"I will admit, Kenzo is a little stuck on himself, but other than that he's a great guy. "

"I guess. I've yet to see this great guy you speak of. To me, he's an egotistical ass wipe. "

"Tell me how you really feel," Madison joked. "Look, it seems to me like your feelings for Kenzo are more than what you portray them to be. "

"Are you trying to insinuate that I like … like him?" Nik looked at Madison sideways.

"I'm not tryin' to say anything," Madison corrected her. "You like Kenzo, bitch. "

"No the hell I don't. " Nik screwed up her face.

"Yes, you do. You want him to put his man meat in your mouth," Madison teased.

"You are such a dirty whore. " Nik couldn't help but giggle. "Seriously, I don't like Kenzo. I'm in love with Greg. " Nik tried to convince herself.

"Mmm-hmm. I believe you. " Madison smirked.

"Oh, whatever. " Nik got up. "I don't have to prove anything to you. I love Greg. " She pointed her finger. "He's an amazing man. He's everything that I want in a mate. "

"Are you trying to convince me or yourself?" Madison eyed her.

Unwilling to admit that her friend was right; Nik placed her hands on her hips and said, "When did you become such a jerk?"

"Whatever, you just don't like to hear the truth. "

"Oh fuck it. " Nik threw up the middle finger. "I'm done. See you at dinner. "She opened the door.

"I love you too!" Madison yelled after her.

* * *

Under the golden light of the moon the entire wedding party and guests sat along a long wooden table that seated twenty. Over their heads were round yellow light bulbs that lit the wooden tented area. Surrounding them were tiki torches. On the table there were candles and flowers. The cool breeze from the ocean kissed their skin as they all ate a scrumptious meal and sipped wine.

"Mmm, these scallops are delicious," Greg commented, savoring the meal.

"You've said that like ten times already. I think we get it," Nik snapped.

"What is your problem?" Greg whispered so that no one else could hear.

For the last few weeks she'd been a stressed out, tyrannical bitch. Any and everything he said got underneath her skin. Greg tried to be understanding but there was only so much a man could take.

"Nothing, I'm just tired, that's all. " Nik picked at her food.

"Well, don't take it out on me," Greg snapped back.

Noticing the angry look on his face, Nik lovingly wrapped her arms around his neck and kissed his cheek.

"I'm sorry. I've been such a bitch to you. You don't deserve that. " She kissed him again.

"Thank you. " Greg looked into her eyes and kissed her lips softly.

Across the table Kenzo watched Nik and Greg's PDA session and began to feel sick to his stomach. He didn't know why seeing her be affectionate with her man upset him so. Hell, he hadn't even seen her in three years, and nothing about her aggressive, uptight attitude had changed. Yet and still, he couldn't take his eyes off of her or get her out of his head.

She was drop dead gorgeous. The dim light from the candles enhanced her smooth cocoa brown skin. Unlike the Hollywood starlets and groupies he often dated, she was very conservative. But Nik's less-is-more approach to fashion suited her well. She was so pretty that makeup and flashy clothes weren't needed. The simple white maxi dress she wore accentuated every curve of her statuesque frame. Kenzo only wished it was he she was kissing instead of Greg.

"I am trying to eat. " Kenzo threw down his fork.

"And?" Nik shot back.

"And you and your man are making me and everyone else uncomfortable, that's what. "

"You are so full of crap. " Nik curled her upper lip.

"Just think of someone else besides yourself, a'ight?" Kenzo took a gulp of his drink.

"You are so pathetic, and that's coming from somebody who's wearing white after Labor Day. "

"And you're so beautiful I forgot how bad your personality was," Kenzo said. "You know what else? You're so uptight I bet you check your watch during sex. "

Shocked by his remark, Nik gasped for air. "Oh those are fighting words," she yelled standing up. "You must not know about me! I will stab you with this fork!" Nik held the fork up in a stabbing position.

"Oh Jesus. " Madison's mom clutched her chest.

"Okay, that's enough you two!" Madison lost her cool. "Until you can work things out and stop bickering, you two—" she pointed back and forth between them. "—are not welcome to sit at the grown-up table. "

Nik said, "But—"

"But nothing'!" Madison cut her off. "Go!"

"See what you did?" Kenzo griped, scooting his chair back.

"Just shut up!" Nik rolled her eyes, leaving the table.

Pissed that Kenzo had gotten them both kicked out of dinner, Nik angrily stormed into the main house with Kenzo hot on her tail. Without warning, she spun around on her heels, startling him.

"What is your issue? Why do you hate me so much?" She squinted her eyes.

"That's stupid. I don't hate you. You just get on my nerves. "

"Whether I get on your nerves or not, we still have to be around each other for the next few days, so why don't we both put our feelings aside for Madison and Keith; because after this, we won't have to see each other hopefully for another three years. "

"Why don't you just admit it?" Kenzo stepped into her personal space.

"Admit what?" Nik looked at him up and down, backing up.

"That you like me. " Kenzo wrapped his right arm around her waist and pulled her in close.

"Are you high?" Nik laughed. "I can't stand your guts. The sight of your face makes me sick. "

"So you tryna to tell me you don't find me attractive?" Kenzo kissed her neck softly.

Nik's panties instantly became wet.

"No, I've seen better," she lied, savoring the feel of his lips on her skin.

"No you haven't. " He licked her ear.

"Oh my God. You are so vain. " Nik pushed him off of her.

"Just kiss me so we can get this over with. " Kenzo adjusted his hard dick.

"I don't wanna kiss you. I have a man. " Nik tried to calm herself down.

"That lame. You don't want him. "

"No, what I don't want is you. " She rolled her eyes so hard her head began to hurt. "Now I'm going back to finish my meal. Please don't ever do that again. " She stepped past him quickly and went back outdoors.

Back at the table, Nik apologized to everyone and resumed eating. She prayed that how terrified she felt on the inside didn't resonate on her face because her stomach was doing summersaults. Every square inch of her body wanted to give in to temptation and take it there with Kenzo. But if she slept with him, Nik would only become another notch on his belt. He'd never make her his woman or hold her close to him at night. He wouldn't ease her worries or share his deepest darkest secrets.

He'd only break her heart like he'd done to all of the rest. Besides, they were complete opposites. She was a sharp tongued, straight lace, do-gooder and he was a playboy without a care in the world. Nik was with whom she belonged. Greg was everything on paper she'd prayed for and more. He was successful, smart, and responsible. Unfortunately for Nik, all of the great qualities about Greg didn't get her wet at night.

* * *

The clock on the wall struck 1:00 AM as Kenzo bent Laila over the foot of his bed and slid his thick, ten-inch dick into her. She was delightfully wet and her body was devilishly thick. But her supple breasts and Serena Williams ass couldn't keep thoughts of Nik out his mind. All Kenzo could imagine was her precious mouth moaning his name. He wished it was her he was hitting from behind, but Nik wanted no parts of him.

She was the one woman on earth who saw through his bull-shit. She made him take responsibility for his immoral ways. She made him think about a life where only they existed. She was the only woman who made him think of settling down. With her, he wanted the all-American lifestyle where they had a house with a white picket fence, two kids, and a dog. But Nik couldn't see past his snarky comments and the hundreds of women he'd bedded. Determined to push thoughts of her from his mind, Kenzo gripped Laila's waist and stroked her middle hard, but slow.

"Mmm … yeah! Give me that big dick, Daddy! Yeah!" Laila clawing the sheets.

She was so wet Kenzo thought he was drowning. Laila had the type of pussy a man could get lost in, but after their rendezvous he'd discard her like he'd done all of the other women he'd dicked down. With his eyes focused on her butt, Kenzo built up speed, causing her ass cheeks to jiggle against his pelvis. The erotic vision before him turned him on to the fullest. There was nothing he found sexier than a fat ass shaking. Enthralled by her moans, Kenzo began pounding her pussy until she screamed. He was hitting it so hard the headboard knocked against the wall. Little did he know, but the woman he fantasized about was on the other side of the wall listening to it all.

* * *

"This cannot be happening. I swear I have been transported to hell. " Nik turned onto her stomach and covered her head with a pillow.

"Babe, it will be over soon," Greg tried to reason.

"No—" Nik uncovered her face. "—it won't. We'll die before they tire out. "

"You are so dramatic. " Greg laughed. "How about instead of stressing off of them, we get into a little fun ourselves. " He scooted near her.

"Are you serious?" Nik screwed up her face.

"Yeah. " Greg pulled her close and caressed her butt.

"Do you really think I'm in the mood to have sex with you right now?"

"Apparently not. " Greg rolled over onto his back, disappointed.

"I will be so happy when we're back in New York and this is over with. "Nik huffed.

"You don't think you're over reacting? They're just having sex, something we should be doing. "

"Oh, so it's my fault that they're having sex so loud they sound like a herd of cows?"

"I'm not saying that?"

"Then what are you sayin', Greg?"

"Can you stop being so defensive. All I'm saying is we're on this gorgeous island and all you've done since we've gotten here is complaining about Kenzo every five seconds. " He pointed out.

Nik laid still. For once she didn't have a rebuttal. Everything Greg said was on point. She was so consumed with Kenzo's every move that she couldn't even enjoy herself. But how could she when every second of the day thoughts of him consumed her? No matter how much she liked to pretend that the very sight of him got underneath her skin, she secretly craved his attention.

She yearned to be the one who screamed out his name in the still of night. She wanted to feel his dick slide in and out her wetness as her body begged for more. For years she'd died to know exactly what was it about him that drove women mad. In all of her days, Nik had never experienced that kind of animalistic, self-indulgent, mind-bending, toe-tingling type of attraction; not even with Greg. Nothing about him or their life together excited her. He was the kind of man she'd been bred to marry, but Nik craved more. She just didn't know if she had the balls to go after it.

* * *

It was 8:00 AM and the sun was in full bloom and warming up the atmosphere. Kenzo had just finished his morning workout. After showering and throwing on a crisp V-neck tee shirt, army fatigue shorts, and flip-flops, he headed outdoors for breakfast. That morning they'd be having breakfast on the beach. The chef had prepared a mouth-watering array of food, including his favorites:- French toast, fresh fruit, eggs Benedict, and bacon. After his two and half hour sexapade with Laila and not nutting, Kenzo had built up quite an appetite.

It was the first time in his life he hadn't been able to perform to his fullest potential and he blamed it all on Nik. If it hadn't been for her constantly being on his mind, he might've been able to enjoy himself. But because of her he didn't have an orgasm or sleep a wink. The only thing that somewhat put him at ease was working out, but even after that he still felt wound up. To Kenzo's surprise, as he reached the beach, Keith and several others were eating breakfast. Kenzo naturally assumed that everyone else would still be asleep.

"What, you up?" Keith greeted him with a pound. "I just knew you were still asleep after last night. "

"What you mean?" Kenzo fixed himself a plate.

"Don't act like you don't know. You and ol' babe. Madison and I could hear y'all all the way from our room. "

"Aw damn, my bad. " Kenzo grinned.

"You good. We was gettin' it in too. " Keith laughed. "I'm sure Nik gon' have something to say, though. "

"What else is new?" Kenzo poured himself a glass of orange juice.

"Speaking of the devil, there she goes now. " Keith pointed with his head.

Kenzo looked over his shoulder and spotted her swimming toward the shore. The sight was something reminiscent of a James Bond movie. The immaculate white sand, turquoise blue water and clear sky complemented her ravishing cocoa physique well. Kenzo was totally mesmerized. As she approached the shore and came up from underneath the water, trickles of water dripped down her body like rain. Her long, wet hair clung to the nape of her neck while the blue, bandeau bikini top and bottoms she wore exposed her hard nipples and the imprint of her pussy lips.

She was absolute perfection. Kenzo had never seen her so at ease and comfortable in her own skin. She was a naturally beautiful woman, but to him she'd never been sexier. But all of that washed away when he saw Greg approach her with a white towel. Kenzo watched in utter disdain as he kissed her lips and wiped her body down.

"I know she fine," Keith said, interrupting his thoughts. "But I ain't know she was that fine. "

"What you talking about?" Kenzo blinked.

"You're pouring orange juice all over the table. "

"Fuck. " Kenzo jumped, immediately catching himself. He had no idea that he'd poured half of the orange juice on the table

"I'll get that for you, sir. " One of the maids took the pitcher from his hand.

"I'm sorry. "

"It's okay. " The maid blushed.

"Go eat your breakfast. " Keith patted Kenzo on the back. "I'mma go check on my soon-to-be-wife. "

"A'ight, I'll catch up wit you in a second. " Kenzo went over to the table and sat down.

Dressed in a sheer flyaway cover up, Nik walked over to the buffet station fully refreshed from her swim. After a sleepless night she felt invigorated. She'd made it up in her mind that she would not fall into the trap of bickering with Kenzo or allowing his antics to affect her. She was going to bask in everything Neckar Island had to offer and devote all of her energy to Greg, who had gone back to their room.

Their relationship was on life support, and if she didn't try her hardest, what they had was sure to die. Once she was done fixing her plate, Nik walked over to the table. To her displeasure she quickly realized that the only available seat was next to Kenzo. Inhaling deeply she placed her plate on the table. "Good morning," she spoke as the wind exposed her stomach and thighs.

Taking in the close-up view of her body, Kenzo looked into her eyes and said, "What's up?"Despite their constant battle he decided to be a gentleman and pull out her chair.

"Thank you," Nik said, surprised. Seated, she said a silent prayer to God and took a small bite of her croissant.

"So did you sleep well?" Kenzo said.

"Um, no. Somebody kept me up all night. " Nik smirked.

"My bad. "He chuckled.

"I'm sure Laila isn't. Home girl gon' need a wheelchair after the way you put it on her. "

"That was a good one. " Kenzo dropped his head and laughed. "But what makes you think it was Laila?"

"Oh, I wouldn't be surprised if it wasn't. "

"Well, it was. " Kenzo confessed so she wouldn't think any more less of him.

"Look, who you sleep with is none of my business. "Nik cut her eyes at him.

"So you still wanna pretend like you ain't feelin' me?" Kenzo turned and looked at her.

"Whether I like you or not doesn't matter," Nik whispered. "I have a boyfriend and you just slept with one of the other brides-maids less than ten hours ago. "

"That didn't mean nothing. "Kenzo insisted.

"Like that makes it better," she scoffed. "Look, you're hand-some and you're a mega movie star, I get it. But we don't have anything in common. Our blind date three years ago proved it. "

"Exactly, that was three years ago and so what if we don't share the same likes and dislikes. Haven't you ever heard the phrase opposites attract? Clearly we attract. "

"The fact that we're even having this conversation is too much for me. I'mma good girlfriend and I don't do things like this. " Nik tried to steady her heart.

"But we haven't even done anything yet. " Kenzo came closer.

"That's the key word, yet. I can't hurt Greg. I just can't. " Nik quickly got up from the table and raced up the pathway leading back to the main house.

Her life was spiraling out of control and Kenzo was the cause of it. He was making her feel things she shouldn't, and if he kept it up, she was sure to act on her forbidden feelings.

THREE

"I don't wanna feel my legs"
Kelly Rowland, Motivation

The following day was the day of the long awaited bachelor/bachelorette party and Nik was a total wreck. She'd been so busy going over the last minute details that when it was time for her to start getting dressed, she ended up hating her hair and outfit. Distressed, she stood in front of the bathroom mirror in tears. The party was in full swing and she was in no way, shape, or form presentable enough to attend. As she cried her eyes out, she heard a sudden knock on the door.

"Yes?" She blew her nose.

"Nik, it's me, Maddie. Is everything okay?" Maddie eased into the room.

"No. " Nik sniffled, coming out of the bathroom. "Look at me. ' She held up her arms.

"I look a hotmess. com. My hair won't stay straight and my dress has a stain on it. "

"Okay, calm down. " Madison held her by the arms. "All of this can be fixed. Since your hair won't stay straight because of the heat, you'll just wear it curly; and as far as your outfit is concerned, I have the perfect dress you can borrow. "

"I am so sorry, Maddie. " Nik cried even harder. "You shouldn't be up here dealing with my drama. You should be enjoying your party. "

"Well, there is no party if you're not there. So come on, let's get you pretty. " Madison led her back into the bathroom.

Almost an hour later, she and Nik sauntered outside to another one of the estate's outdoor dining areas. Nik was pleasantly pleased with how everything turned out. To create a club like environment, she had strobe lights, white leather couches, and chairs flown in. Tons of white flowers were everywhere, and to keep the party hype, a DJ spun nothing but hip hop and reggae records.

But the exquisite décor was only a backdrop for Nik. Nothing or no one, not even Maddie, held a candle to her. It was as if time stood still as soon as she entered the room. You could almost hear a pin drop. All eyes were on her.

Her hair was filled with an abundance of tight curls and Madison had created a sultry, bronze look with her makeup. To complete the sexy look, she rocked a hot pink, open-back maxi dress with spaghetti straps that crisscrossed and tied in the back. The body-hugging dress accentuated her full breasts and clung to her hips. Kenzo didn't know if he could contain himself. He had to have her and that night he wasn't going to take no for an answer.

"Girl, you doing it tonight. " Maddie winked at her before heading over to Keith.

Slightly uncomfortable by the male attention she was receiving, Nik folded her arms across her chest until she locked eyes with Greg. Smiling from ear to ear, she placed her arms by her side, hoping he'd like how she looked.

"What took you so long?" he said, giving her peck on the cheek.

"Girl problems, that's all. "

"What's up with the outfit?" He stepped back and looked at her.

"You don't like it?" Nik held her breath.

"I mean, don't you think it's a bit much? You're showing a lot of skin. It kind of looks a bit trashy. " Greg tuned up his face.

"Trashy? I got this dress from Maddie. "

"That explains it. "He turned up the corner of his mouth.

"Whoa, whoa, whoa, pump your brakes, homeboy. That's my best friend you're talking about. " Nik was heated.

"I'm just sayin'. You look kind of whorish. "

"Wow," Nik scoffed, feeling two feet tall. "This conversation is officially over. " She pushed pass him.

"Nik, wait!" He tried to stop her.

"No, I'm good!" She continued to walk away.

Thoroughly upset, Nik grabbed a glass of Rosé champagne and guzzled it down. Normally she didn't drink, but tonight she felt like letting loose. She was so sick of Greg pointing his nose down at her. For three years he'd corrected her speech, instructed her on what to wear, eat, and who to socialize with. Nik was over it. She was a grown-ass woman, and she was done with allowing him to control her life. It was time for her to do her and whoever didn't like it could kiss her ass.

With her second drink in hand, Nik took to the dance floor. The sweet sound of Carl Thomas's hit song Summer Rain persuaded her hips to sway to the beat. Already on the dance floor with Laila, Kenzo focused his attention on Nik. The wind was softly whistling, causing her dress to blow.

Each time the wind blew and the hem of her dress raised, his eyes zeroed in on her long, lean legs. Nik had legs like a supermodel. All he could envision was laying her down on the sand and placing himself in between her beautiful legs. Tired of watching her from afar, Kenzo—without notice—stepped away from Laila and joined Nik.

"Hey. " Laila pouted.

But Kenzo didn't even stop to respond.

"You gon' hurt somebody in that dress," he said, taking Nik by the hand.

"You like?" Her face lit up.

"Hell yeah. "They began to two-step like a couple in love.

* * *

"Well, look-a-here. " Madison tapped Keith on the shoulder so he could see.

"Looks like somebody's getting along," he replied.

"Yeah," Madison agreed. "A little too much if you ask me. Greg is pissed. "

Only Greg wasn't pissed. He was livid. Not only had Nik disregarded his feelings about her outfit, but she was now parading around like a cheap floozy. The way she was behaving was embarrassing. Enough was enough. Slamming his drink down on the table, Greg stormed over to Nik and grabbed her by the arm.

"Uh-oh, it's about to go down. " Madison cracked her knuckles ready to fight.

"Fall back. That's their business. " Keith pulled her back.

* * *

"Yo. " Kenzo placed his hand on Greg's chest pushing him back. "You a'ight?"

"Obviously, I'm not and you need to mind your business. This is between Nicolette and me. "

"It's cool," Nik assured Kenzo.

"Really, Nik?" Greg looked at her surprised. "Since when did you two become such good friends?"

"Look, if you wanna talk, let's go talk. " Nik was fed up.

Seconds later she and Greg stood silently on the beach watching the wave's crash upon the shore.

"You wanted to talk, so talk," she finally said.

"What's going on with you? Since the morning of our flight you've been different. " Greg stared at the sand.

"Different how, Greg?'Cause I'm not obeying your every word? 'Cause what you say isn't gospel to me anymore or—"

"No!" Greg cut her off. "'Cause you're in love with Kenzo!"

"That's ridiculous. " Nik shook her head.

"It's written all over your face! Everyone can see it, except you!"

Unable to face him, Nik turned her back to him and gazed up at the moon. Tears burned the brim of her eyes. Her voice wanted desperately to scream that Greg's words were a lie, but they weren't. She was over the moon for Kenzo and she could no longer hide it, nor did she want to. She wanted to experience what it felt like to lose control. It was time to allow herself to be open to the uncertainty of the unknown.

With Kenzo nothing would be ordinary or boring. With him she could be her true self and not pretend that she was perfect. With him she could let her hair down and breathe, but the fact still remained that although Kenzo brought out the best in her, he was a known player.

"So you're going to deny it and turn your back to me?" Greg said in disbelief.

"You're right. " Nik faced him. "I do have feelings for him. "Suddenly she felt as if

a weight had been lifted off of her chest. She knew that telling Greg the truth was relationship suicide, but it had to be done.

"So where does that leave us?" He had a hard time digesting her confession.

"I guess that means its over. " Nik swallowed hard.

"Wow," Greg said astonished. "After three years, this is how it ends?"

"Let's be honest, Greg. Things between us haven't been good for a while. You want something from me that I can't give you and vice versa. I'm tired of acting like I'm satisfied with our relationship when I'm not, and I know you can't honestly say you don't feel the same way. "

Pushing his anger to the side, Greg took a deep breath and exhaled slowly. "You're right. I'm not happy. I just thought that maybe after some time things would change. "

"Me too, but it hasn't and it won't," Nik replied.

"Look, there's a boat heading to the mainland in an hour, I'm going to catch it," Greg said.

"You're leaving? No. I don't want you to do that. This was supposed to be your vacation too. "

"Nah, I think its best I leave. If I stay, it'll only be awkward and neither of us wants that. "

Tears fell from Nik's eyes at the speed of lightning. She knew it was best for the both for them if he left, but she never imagined their story ending this way.

"Stop. " Greg wiped her tears away. "Everything's okay. We're doing what's best. "

Nik was choked up but she nodded her head.

"I'mma go pack. " He placed his hand inside of his pocket.

"Okay. " Nik bit the inside of her lip.

Oblivious to the fact that Kenzo was coming her way, Nik watched as Greg's back faded into the dark night.

"You a'ight?" Kenzo said to her from behind.

"Yeah. " She spun around.

"You don't look a'ight. " Kenzo examined her tear stained face.

"Did he put his hands on you?'

"No. We broke up. "

"Damn, for real?" Kenzo said with a huge grin on his face.

"Don't hide your true feelings," Nik said sarcastically.

"What? He wasn't the man for you. You belong to me. " He pulled her into embrace.

"This is crazy. You and I are never going to work. "

"Stop being so damn scary. Let go and allow me to like you. "

"You like me so much but you just slept with Laila. "

"Why you bringing up ol' shit? I only did that 'cause it was convenient and she was there. And besides, we don't need to get off into all of that. I'm diggin' the hell outta you, and I wanna see what this can lead to. I want you to be mine and I'm not taking no for an answer. "

Nik swallowed the huge lump in her throat. This was it, the moment where she either stayed on course or ventured out into the unknown. Ready to experience uninhibited bliss, she allowed her heart to open up to the possibility of being truly in like with some-one. While gazing into Kenzo's tranquil eyes, Nik draped her arms around his neck then kissed his lips. Passionately, their tongues intertwined.

Nik felt as if she were floating on clouds made of air. For years she'd secretly watched Kenzo's movies and wondered what his tongue tasted like. Now Nik new first hand that it tasted like wine. Enthralled by his touch, she gladly allowed him to untie the back of her dress. Fully exposed to the elements, she let the top of the dress fall to her waist.

As Kenzo placed sensual kisses from her neck down to her breasts, Nik closed her eyes and listened to the roaring waves before her. She didn't know what was more captivating, the sound of the ocean or the feel of Kenzo's tongue flickering on her hard nipples. Each flick sent jolts of electricity through her stomach. As she reeled from his kisses, Kenzo held each of her breasts in his hand and sucked on her nipples mercilessly.

Her coffee-colored skin felt like the finest silk against his tongue. He couldn't wait to explore every crevice of her body. Easing his way further south of the border, Kenzo pulled her dress and thong off. For a second he sat back on his knees and admired her goddess like physique. Every square inch of her was perfect and further proved that she was the woman of his dreams.

Not wanting to waste another second, he swiftly undressed as well. Completely naked, he gently laid Nik down on the sand. Finally, his fantasy was about to come true. Nik couldn't wait for him to taste her and Kenzo couldn't wait either. Once his tongue met with her clit they both were satisfied. Nik was in heaven. Kenzo's tongue was wreaking havoc on her pussy.

"Kenzo," she moaned, kneading her nipples. "Baby ... ooh. "

"Damn, you taste good. " Kenzo thumbed her clit while sucking the lips of her pussy.

He was driving Nik insane. She couldn't control herself. Moans of pleasure were escaping through her lips and into the night air.

"Ooh, baby, fuck me," she begged. "Fuck me, Kenzo … please fuck me. Ooh, I can't take it anymore, fuck me. "

Happy to oblige her request, Kenzo softly kissed her navel, breasts, and lips before smoothly sliding his rock hard dick into her wet slit. The first thrust was mind-blowing. Kenzo couldn't get enough of her. Her pussy was like black voodoo. The harder and deeper he stroked, the more he didn't want the moment to end.

"Shit," Nik said as he flipped her over.

At that very second, she knew she wouldn't be able to feel her legs the next day. Digging her hands into the sand, she matched his thrust and threw her ass back into his shaft. Loving the way she worked it, Kenzo slapped her ass.

"Kenzo!" Nik screamed totally turned on.

"You like that?" He groaned, pulling her hair.

"Yes, don't stop!" Nik panted as her thighs began to shake.

She knew that she was being loud and that someone might overhear, but Kenzo had her sewn up. Whatever he wanted of her she'd happily give. She'd be his slave, his freak, whatever. Determined to make the most of the opportunity, she spun around and pushed him onto his back. His thick, creamy dick was standing at full attention. Obsessed by the sight, Nik ran her tongue across her upper lip.

Before Kenzo knew it she'd taken all of him in her mouth. His long rod slid in and out of her mouth with velvet ease. While her tongue manipulated Kenzo's dick to the point he was almost experiencing convulsions, Nik played with her clit. She was so wet her fingers kept slipping.

"Let me taste it. " Kenzo pulled her onto him.

In the sixty-nine position, Nik resumed sucking his dick with reckless abandon. Kenzo had been with a lot of women, but never in his life had any woman devoured his dick like Nik. The farther she pushed him into her mouth the further she wanted to go. The way Kenzo was licking her clit didn't help much either. The sensation was sending her over the edge. The orgasm that was building inside of her was so explosive she couldn't think straight.

As she licked the tip of his Kenzo's dick, she could tell by the stiffness of his penis that at any moment he was about to nut. Nik had never allowed a man to come in her mouth, but for some reason she couldn't see Kenzo cumming anywhere else.

"Baby, I'm gettin' ready to come. " He kissed her butt cheeks.

"Me too," Nik said, coming up for air.

Taking all of him back into her mouth she eagerly bobbed her head up and down his shaft until Kenzo's love juices filled her mouth and slid down her throat. Massaging her butt cheeks Kenzo licked her pussy lips until every sweet drop of juice lathered his tongue. Spent, Nik wiped her mouth and placed her head on Kenzo's chest. With one of his arms wrapped around her neck, Kenzo stroked his hard dick with his free hand.

"What are you doing?" Nik said, joining in.

"Gettin' ready for round two. "

* * *

The next morning, after making love until the sun came up, Kenzo and Nik lay on the beach wrapped in each other's arms. It was the day of the wedding and they would have to get up soon, but neither of them wanted to move. They were completely smitten with each other.

"You know everybody's probably lookin' for us," Nik said, still high from their all-night love affair.

"Yeah, I know. You ready to head back up?"

"Yeah, let's get dressed. " Nik sat up and put her dress back on.

"Last night was crazy. " Kenzo pulled up his shorts.

"Last night was delicious," Nik said with a devilish grin on her face.

"So what now? Where do we go from here?" Kenzo said fully dressed.

"Let's just take it one day at a time. " Nik walked up to him and put her arms around his waist. "I'm not going anywhere. Like you said, I belong to you and after last night, you for damn sure belong to me. "

Other books by: